The Cardinal
& the Crane

Alice Kanaka

This book is a work of fiction. The events and characters portrayed are imaginary. Their resemblance, if any, to real-life counterparts is entirely coincidental. Actual places are used in a fictional context and this story is in no way portraying any real events, staff, internal workings, or management.

Table of Contents

Chapter 1

Sam sat quietly, trying to slow her racing heart and unclench her muscles. She squeezed her eyes shut and bit her lip to gain control of her emotions. Taking a deep breath, she said a quick prayer and glanced at her cousin. "Jack?"

"Yes?" He didn't open his eyes.

"We need to talk."

"I know."

"I've never even been on an airplane, and I've missed you so much. I should be ecstatic, but instead, I'm miserable."

"I'm sorry, Sam," Jack mumbled.

"If you didn't want me here, why did you invite me?"

He opened his eyes and looked at her. "I did want you here. I *do* want you here."

"You're not acting like it."

"I don't know *how* to act. I don't know how to get past everything that's happened."

Sam smiled sadly. "Remember when you came to Santo Milagro to find my dad, and we realized we were cousins?"

"I do. We had a lot of fun together."

"Since we thought we were cousins, there was no question of anything else, and you fell in love with Ally. Remember?"

"Yes." He lowered his eyes as he was hit by an unexpected rush of grief.

"We're still the same people, Jack. We're still cousins and can still be best friends."

"But we're not really cousins, and you got married."

"Does that matter? We can still have great adventures together, starting with this one.

"I can't stand you treating me like a stranger. Three weeks of this will kill me."

"I'll do better. I've just been stuck in my own head. Seeing you again and worrying about meeting my mom's family is a lot to process." Jack took her hand and smiled. "This will be the adventure of a lifetime."

Sam squeezed his hand and grinned. "Want to watch a movie?"

"You pick one. I'll see if I can flag down the flight attendant."

"I doubt they have Modelo Negra."

"No problem. I'm flexible."

Sam laughed and began looking through the movie selections. She knew what kind of movies Jack liked and avoided the romcoms.

<hr>

Jack watched Sam out of the corner of his eye, thinking back to the day they first met and how they had just seemed to click. He remembered how he felt about her when he thought they were first cousins and how much fun they had. He was ashamed of his own behavior since he found out she had married. His disappointment and jealousy had overshadowed their relationship to such an extent that he had excised her from his life completely. That hadn't worked; it just made him more miserable.

Now, sitting next to her on the plane, joking and making fun of the movie they were watching, his anxiety decreased considerably. He was still nervous about meeting his mom's family, but at least he was facing it with his best friend at his side.

Taking a sip of his drink, he discovered it was empty. He looked up to find Sam studying his face. "What?"

"You're not watching the movie. And your cup is empty." She waved at the flight attendant.

"Sorry. I'm still nervous. I thought I was just coming to meet my grandparents, but it seems there is also an aunt and uncle and a couple of cousins. I hope someone at least speaks English."

"Have you studied any Japanese?"

"Some very rudimentary things like greetings, numbers, basic sentence structure. Enough to get by in an emergency, perhaps."

"I have a phrase book." She grinned. "Is someone going to pick us up at the airport?"

"Someone will be there." Jack's eyebrows furrowed. "They said something about a train."

<hr>

A small, middle-aged woman was waiting for them outside the customs area, holding a sign that said 'Jack Olivares' in big letters. When Jack approached, she bowed at the waist and began speaking rapidly in Japanese.

"I'm so sorry. Gomenasai. I don't speak Japanese."

She looked perplexed, then pointed to the sign and said, "Jyaku-san desu ne."

"Yes, I'm Jack." Bowing at the waist, he said, "Yoroshiku onegaishimasu."

Sam's eyes got round. "What's that mean?" she whispered.

"It's a greeting. I learned just enough to confuse people." He frowned as the woman took off speaking Japanese again.

She ended with. "No English." She turned her hand upside down and drew her fingers toward her palm several times before turning and leading them down a wide corridor.

Having stopped once to check their luggage at a shipping counter, Jack had dozens of questions and had completely lost his bearings by the time they reached a busy platform. The woman gave them each a ticket and handed Jack a piece of paper before bowing again and backing away.

Jack looked down at the paper, and when he looked up again, she had disappeared into the crowd.

"What's it say?" Sam tried to see the paper he was holding.

"It says Narita Express to Tokyo Station. Kodama shinkansen to Kakegawa. JR Tokaido Line to Iwata."

"Like I said, an adventure. This must be the express train?"

"I wonder where our luggage went."

"Wherever it went, at least we don't have to carry it."

A recorded voice announced the arrival of the train, and the doors quietly slid open.

The inside of the train was clean and silent. Discovering they had reserved seats, they made themselves comfortable.

———

Sam was getting tired of traveling. Exiting the train at Tokyo Station an hour later, she gaped.

"I read somewhere that 500,000 people pass through this station every day," Jack said distractedly. "Come on. It looks like everyone is heading upstairs."

Upstairs, the station was disorienting. Myriad signs, timetables, and ticket gates were further confused by bustling travelers intent on reaching their destinations. Standing frozen in the stream of humanity, Sam looked around until Jack pointed at a sign.

"There. Shinkansen. I think we want to go that way."

"What does shinkansen mean?"

"It's the bullet train. Some of them go as fast as 199 miles per hour."

"What?" She followed him through the labyrinth of corridors until they finally found the platform for Kakegawa. "This is crazy," she said under her breath. "I've never seen such a busy place. It reminds me of a beehive. Should we ask someone if we're on the right platform? We don't even know what's on these tickets. That guy over there looks like he works here."

Sam walked over to the man she had indicated and showed him her ticket. "Is this the right train?"

The man looked at her ticket and pointed, nodding.

Returning to where Jack stood, Sam said, "It's the right place."

Jack's shoulders relaxed slightly. "If I had known we were taking a train by ourselves, I would have done some research."

"Sometimes it's fun to just wing it. What's the worst that could happen?"

"Um, I don't know. We could end up in some city we've never heard of and spend our entire trip trying to find Iwata?"

"It would still be an adventure." Sam elbowed him. "It might be even more fun than meeting the grandparents."

Jack raised one eyebrow.

"I'm just kidding. You know I want to meet them." She laughed. "Here comes the train."

Sam fell asleep once they had gotten settled, and Jack spent the trip lost in thought, snapping to attention an hour and forty minutes later when he heard the announcement for Kakegawa. *Here we go again... I hope they don't have big plans for us this evening. At least Sam got some sleep.* He turned to Sam and put his hand on her shoulder. "Sam? We're here."

Slowly opening her eyes, she looked at him in confusion.

"We're arriving at Kakegawa station. Just one more to go."

"Oh. Gee. I forgot where I was for a minute. I'm so tired."

"I know. Not much longer, I hope."

They wearily boarded a local train for the final leg of their trip and were surprised when the train pulled into Iwata station sixteen minutes later.

As they left the platform, Jack spied another sign with his name on it, but this time, the curvy young woman holding the sign had a blonde bob and was dressed in jeans and a snug t-shirt that read *Jubilo Iwata*.

She grinned and waved when she saw them. "You must be Jack and Sam. I'm Annie. Welcome to Iwata."

Jack glanced around. "I was going to ask how you knew it was us but guess it's rather obvious." He smiled and shook her hand. "The woman who met us at Narita..."

"Yes, sorry about that. She's your aunt's sister. She agreed to meet you because she lives nearby, but she was worried about not speaking English. Was it difficult taking the train?"

"We managed. I'm not sure where our luggage went, though."

"It's already at the house. I'm Takashi's wife, by the way."

"Takashi?"

"Your cousin." Annie smiled kindly. "I'll introduce you to everyone when we get home. It's not far." She led them to a white Toyota Corolla and helped them adjust the seats before pulling away from the curb.

After a short, ten-minute drive, she parked in front of a boxy, two-story house built near the end of a very narrow road.

"This house looks different from the others," Sam commented.

"Land is so expensive here that families rebuild rather than buy new homes. The Akiyama family has lived here for six generations, and the original house was falling apart. Your uncle and Takashi are at work, but I'll introduce you to Grandma and your aunt, then give you a cultural tour of the house."

Jack had no idea what a cultural tour meant but glanced at Sam and nodded amicably.

Chapter 2

Opening the front door, Annie called, "Tadaima!" and then stopped in the large, tiled entryway to remove her shoes.

"Okaerinasai!" answered two female voices from the next room.

Annie showed Sam and Jack how to place their shoes neatly facing the door and opened a cupboard to retrieve house slippers. "We never wear our shoes inside. I hope you can find some slippers that fit."

As they sorted through the slippers, a small, plump woman with short, permed, black hair rounded the corner carrying a tea towel. She spoke to Annie in Japanese, then addressed Jack, who didn't understand.

"Hajimemashite. Jack desu," he said, bowing low. "Yoroshiku onegaishimasu."

The woman looked very pleased and happily answered him in rapid Japanese.

Jack looked at Annie and said, "That's the extent of my Japanese, I'm afraid. What did she say?"

Laughing, Annie relayed this to the woman. "Jack, this is Etsuko Oba-san. You can call her Oba, which means auntie. She's married to your mother's brother. You'll meet him later. Come meet Grandma."

Annie said something else to Oba, and Jack heard Sam's name.

Oba smiled and led the way into the living room. Grandmother Akiyama sat on the end of a long sofa, watching television and knitting. Her hands moved quickly in an almost unconscious rhythm. Looking up, her face crinkled into dozens of good-natured creases.

7

Her wispy, white hair floated around her face, and Jack could see the resemblance to his mother. Setting her knitting aside, she held out her hands. "Jyaku-kun."

Jack took her hands as she carefully studied his face.

"Jack, this is your obaa-san. She's been very excited to meet you."

"Why are the aunt and grandma called the same thing?" Sam asked.

"No, there is only one 'a' sound for aunt and two for grandma. Oba-san and Obaa-san, see?"

"Can I call them that too?"

"Of course." Annie spoke with Grandma and interpreted for Jack. "Obaa-san said to tell you she's pleased you have come to visit, and she hopes you will be comfortable. I'll show you around so you know where things are and what to do with them."

"Please thank her for me, Annie. I'm very happy to finally meet my family."

⋅⋅⋖◦∞◦⋗⋅⋅

Annie took them on a short tour of the house. The most notable room, which took some explanation, was the bathroom.

A second set of slippers sat inside the door to the toilet, and Annie explained that regular house slippers were not to be worn in the bathroom. "Since there are three of us, we may need to make a small exception. This door" —she opened a clear folding door on the left wall— "leads to the bath. The bathtub is used by the entire family, and the water can be reheated." She lifted the cover and showed them the short, deep tub and the heating element. "Everyone washes first, then soaks in the tub. Just sit on this stool by the spigot, soap up, and rinse with the bowls. When we rebuilt the house, we updated the bathroom so there's a shower hose. It makes it a lot easier."

Sam was fascinated. "Who empties the water and cleans the bathtub?"

"Takashi's mother and I take turns."

"I can help, too, while we're here. Will you show me how?"

"Japanese families frown on guests doing housework."

"Don't be silly. We're family, and we'll be here for a long time."

"I'll ask her, okay? I don't want to upset her."

Sam furrowed her brow but nodded. "What about towels?"

"There's one in your room. I'll show you. When you're done with it, put it in this hamper. Ba-ba and Ji-ji's room is over there. The stairs are getting difficult for them." She pointed to a set of sliding paper doors, across a short hallway, to the left of the bathroom. "It's a tatami room like yours."

"Tatami?" Sam said at the same time Jack asked, "Ba-ba and Ji-ji?"

"Sorry. It's like a nickname for Obaa-san and Ojii-san."

Annie led them to a second set of doors between the grandparents' room and the entryway. Sliding them open, she said, "This is a traditional tatami room. We use it for a guest room and for entertaining company. When it's not in use, the doors are left open, and the family shrine is in here."

Sam looked around. A short, square table and cushions sat to the left near the window, and two single futons were laid out, ready to sleep in. She crouched down and touched the floor. It was a light brown color, laid out in rectangles, and felt soft underfoot.

"That's tatami. It's made from natural materials, like woven rush straw."

An additional set of sliding doors, papered identically to the surrounding walls were set in the opposite wall, and a shrine was mounted on a table to the right, facing the window. Just inside the door sat their suitcases.

"What's through there?" Sam asked. She pointed to the papered doors.

"That's where the futons are usually kept, but this room is yours during your stay, so you can leave them out. Why don't you two get settled, and dinner will be ready soon."

"Thank you very much, Annie. I feel like we're causing a great deal of trouble. Please let us know if there's anything we can do to help."

"No worries," Annie said. "You are making Ba-ba so happy." She smiled at Jack. "When you hear someone call 'gohan', it means dinner's ready." Annie left the room and quietly slid the rice paper doors behind her.

Turning to Jack, Sam widened her eyes. "Huge learning curve."

"I'll say. I feel bad causing so much extra work. At least our suitcases magically arrived so we can give everyone their gifts."

"I wonder what we'll have for dinner."

"Hungry as usual." Jack laughed, opening his suitcase.

Sam opened hers, too, and they carefully extracted their gifts.

"Tadaima!" called male voices outside their room.

"Okaeri!" answered three female voices.

A few minutes later, Oba called, "Gohan!"

Feeling nervous once again, Jack grabbed Sam's hand and gave it a squeeze before crossing the hall to the living room. I wish I had learned more Japanese before I came. They all seem so kind. He stopped at the entrance and looked around. Now, eight people filled the room, including him and Sam, and it seemed much smaller. His grandfather had joined his grandmother on the sofa, and he wondered where he had been earlier.

Annie approached. "Jack, Sam, this is Grandfather. You can call him Ojii-san. And this is Uncle Junichi or Oji. Just like grandma and auntie, there is a single 'i' for uncle and two for grandpa. And this is your cousin, Takashi. You can just call him by his first name."

About the same height as Annie and a head taller than his parents, he approached Jack. "Hello. I am Takashi. You can call me Taka if my name is hard."

"We'll see." Jack smiled. "We brought omiyage. It was in our suitcases."

"Great. We open after dinner."

Oba and Annie busily shuttled food to the large wooden table. The dining area was slightly raised, a step above the living room, and the table sat inside an open, rectangular area that created a bench. Everyone sat on pillows around the table with their legs underneath.

Once they were seated, they said, "Itadakimasu," in unison, and picked up their chopsticks.

Jack turned to Takashi and asked if he could repeat that.

"I-ta-da-ki-masu," Takashi said. "Means thank you, food."

"Like bon appétit," Annie added.

Jack and Sam repeated, "Itadakimasu."

"After dinner, you say 'gochisousamadeshita' or just 'gochisou' if you can't remember the whole thing." Annie grinned.

"I think my brain might explode," Sam said. She watched the others eat and tried to copy what they were doing, but she kept dropping her food.

Jack laughed and handed her a fork before promptly dropping his fish in his lap. "Maybe I should use a fork too."

He vaguely remembered eating this type of meal when his mother was alive.

Each person had a bowl of rice along with other small bowls of pickled vegetables and meat and a bowl of miso soup. Everything was delicious.

The cleanup must be terrible. Perhaps Sam and I can offer to help.

When everyone was finished, Oba and Annie took the dishes into the kitchen and returned with small, rectangular pieces of cake.

Jack tasted his, and to his surprise, it tasted very fresh and not too sweet. *A wonderful palate cleanser.*

"Gochisousamadeshita," everyone said.

"Slowly, please," Jack said.

"Go-chi-so-oo-sama-deshita," Takashi said.

"Gochisousamadeshita," Jack and Sam repeated. "May Sam and I do the dishes?"

"Oh, no. You're guests. Why don't you hand around your omiyage if you like? Oba and I will do the dishes."

Oba looked at Annie with her eyebrows raised in question, and when Annie interpreted, she shook her head vigorously. "No, no dishes." She hurriedly cleared the table and rushed into the kitchen, which was separated from the dining area by a half wall so she could still see what was happening around the table.

Jack and Sam handed out their gifts and watched anxiously as the family opened them. They needn't have worried. Each family member exclaimed over their gift, which was only polite but pleased Jack immensely. He and Sam had shopped separately, but combined, they had come up with a nice selection of southwestern snacks, jewelry, and knick-knacks.

Takashi looked at Sam and said, "Please take a bath."

Sam became very still and glanced at Jack, surreptitiously sniffing at her underarm.

"He is offering it to you first," Annie said. "We were going to take you out for a drink, but I told him you were probably exhausted."

"Oh!" Sam chuckled. "I thought perhaps I was getting ripe. Could you show me again how to heat the water?"

"Don't worry. It's already hot. I hope you enjoy it."

Sam left to take her bath, and Takashi offered Jack a beer.

"I don't know. If Sam smells beer on me and she doesn't get one, I might be in trouble."

Jack was joking, but Takashi missed that and worriedly said, "Of course she can have."

They went to bed early, but Sam's eyes popped open in the middle of the night. She looked at the clock, then over at Jack, who was sleeping peacefully. *Three o'clock. Why am I awake at three o'clock?* She got up and dressed as quietly as she could. Slowly sliding their doors open, she tiptoed to the front entrance, slipped on her shoes, and opened the door a crack.

The air outside was warmer than New Mexico in late April. Stepping into the dark silence, she could imagine herself at home on her ranch. She stood and listened. The air was so still, she imagined she could hear the ocean. She smelled it, too, and wondered if she was being fanciful. *Maybe I'm dreaming.*

She wanted to take a walk but was worried about leaving the front door unlocked. *Was it locked when I opened it?* She couldn't remember. Her mind wandered as she sat on the front step, absorbing the silence. *I wonder what Tom is doing. I miss him.* She pictured her husband's unruly brown hair and his lively blue eyes, not as they looked when she left but as they looked on their wedding day. She wanted to call him but was afraid of what he might say.

She was startled when the front door opened, and Jack stepped outside.

"What are you doing out here?"

She shrugged. "Just enjoying the cool air and the quiet. Look at all the stars."

"Does it make you homesick?"

"Not yet." She smiled. "What time is it?"

"It's almost four."

"Did I wake you?"

"No. It's jet lag. The time difference takes a while to get used to."

"I didn't think of that. I was exhausted and couldn't figure out why I woke up so early."

"Even a few hours can disrupt your body clock. Sixteen hours can really wreak havoc. It's noon at home."

"How long does it take for your body to adjust?"

"Probably two or three days."

Sam rested her elbows on her thighs and her head in her hands. "Should we try to go back to sleep?"

"I think it might be pointless. Want to take a walk?"

"I do, but I didn't want to leave the door unlocked."

"Don't worry. Annie told me they never lock it unless they all go somewhere. Which way do you want to go?"

"I want to find the water. Let's try that way." Sam rose and pointed to the left.

A few houses down, a narrow path led up a slight hill to the right. The path gradually disappeared, covered in sand. As they descended, they could see a vast body of water glimmering in the moonlight, and they heard the gentle rolling of waves rushing up onto the beach.

"It's beautiful," Sam whispered. "Let's take our shoes off." She sat in the sand and removed her shoes, placing her socks inside to keep them dry, and Jack followed suit.

"Where are your boots?" he asked with a grin.

"I didn't hear anything about horses here, so I didn't bring them."

Laughing, Jack said, "I'm glad you didn't dye your hair, or I might not have recognized you."

"Very funny." Sam punched his arm lightly. "I might have if I had time. I wasn't sure what kind of reception I'd get with bright red hair."

"I'm kind of surprised no one has mentioned it, actually, but then people here are very polite."

"They are. I wish I could speak Japanese."

"Me too. Maybe we can study before our next visit."

They walked to the water's edge and rolled up their pant legs. "Brr. It's cold!" Sam said.

Wading in the surf, Sam kicked the water. "You think we'll be able to visit again?"

"Sure. And maybe they can visit us too."

"I like your family. It seems almost like a different world here, doesn't it?"

"Yeah. We need to look at a map. How did we end up on the coast?"

Sam shrugged. "How long 'til breakfast? Do they drink coffee here?"

"Uh oh." Jack laughed. "I sure hope so."

Chapter 3

Sam and Jack ran into Takeshi on their way back to the house. "Where you went?" he asked, jogging in place as they approached.

"We just went for a walk," Jack said. "Jet lag."

"Jetto lagu?"

"We woke up at night because of the time difference."

"Ah. I understand. I run every day. I will be return for breakfast." He gave them a wave and jogged down the street in the direction they had come.

Entering the house and stowing their shoes, they turned right into the family room.

"Ohayou gozaimasu!" Oba said.

"Ohayou!" Annie echoed her. "Are you ready for breakfast?"

"Ohayou," Jack said. "I think we might be."

"Have you been out for a walk?"

"We walked to the beach. Are we on the Pacific coast?"

"We are." Annie smiled. "Be careful in the water here. The locals swim, but there's a strong undertow. Have a seat. Would you like some coffee?"

Jack grinned as Sam happily bounced on her toes. "Coffee! Yes, please."

"Oba usually makes rice, fish, and miso soup for breakfast, but I prefer toast. What would you like?"

"I'll have the toast, please," Sam said. "I think it might go better with coffee."

"I didn't think of that, but I'll try the full breakfast anyway."

"Now I feel bad," Sam said.

"You can try mine and maybe have it tomorrow."

"Good idea." Sam reverently accepted the cup of coffee Annie offered and took a sip. "Oh, coffee, how I have missed you." She sighed blissfully. "Are you sure there's nothing we can do to help?"

"No, not at the moment. Takeshi thought Jack might like to see the family business this morning, and I wondered if you would like to visit my English school. I used to work for a private school, but after we got married, the family set up a studio for me to hold classes in."

Sam glanced at Jack, who nodded. "I would love to."

"We're working this week, but next week is Golden Week, and we'll have the whole week off."

"What's Golden Week?"

"We have three national holidays that week, so most people take a week-long vacation. Before I got married, I used to travel during Golden Week and sometimes went home to see my parents."

"Where's home?" Jack asked with interest.

"I'm from Australia, but this is home now. I've been here almost eight years."

"Wow. No wonder your Japanese is so good," Sam said.

"It's not as good as I'd like it to be, but shoganai ne."

"Shoganai?"

"Um. Kind of like 'that's life' I guess."

Oba called to Annie, and she disappeared into the kitchen, returning with a plate of thick-cut toast and a small salad for Sam, then back into the kitchen, returning once again with a tray for Jack. "One more trip." She went back for her own toast and a cup of coffee.

Sam tried Jack's breakfast and was glad she had chosen the toast. Fish was not her favorite food. His uncle and grandparents joined them at the table about the time Takeshi returned.

"Tadaima!" he called out.

The rest of the family said, "Okaeri."

Sam elbowed Jack and whispered, "I think I'm getting the hang of this."

"Itadakimasu," Oji and Ojii-san said.

"Oops. I forgot that part," Sam mumbled.

When Takeshi sat at the table, he asked Jack if he'd like to join him and his father after breakfast.

"Yes, I would. Very much."

"Itadakimasu." Takeshi picked up his chopsticks.

"What kind of business do you run?"

"It's bento business. We make lunchboxes and delivery."

Jack nodded. Watching the other family members, he mimicked how they ate.

Sam nibbled on her toast; glad she didn't have to worry about trying to eat fish with chopsticks. She was also glad Annie gave her a fork for her salad. "Why are you so good at using chopsticks?" she asked Jack.

"My mom taught me." He smiled.

Oba finally sat at the table with her own breakfast. "Itadakimasu," she said.

"Could I get myself another cup of coffee?" Sam asked Annie.

"I'll get it." She stood and took Sam's cup into the kitchen.

Sam watched her and thought she would feel very bad if they kept waiting on her this way. She couldn't imagine a guest sitting idly for weeks as she tried to meet their every need. That was a lot of pressure. *I'll talk to Annie about it when she shows me her English school.*

After breakfast, everyone said, "Gochisousamadeshita," then rose and went in opposite directions, leaving Oba to clean up the mess.

Sam carried her plate into the kitchen and said, "Please let me help."

"Iie." Oba shook her head stubbornly. "No dishes."

Sam's shoulders slumped, and she went to find Jack.

Jack was already gone, but Annie was speaking on her phone in the entryway, so Sam waited patiently.

Disconnecting, Annie said, "My classes don't start for another two hours. Let's take a walk. There's a park nearby."

She led Sam through narrow streets, just wide enough for a single car to pass through. Many of the homes were built so close together they were almost touching, and shops spilled out of the downstairs onto the sidewalk.

Admiring a display of freshly cut flowers, Sam asked, "Are all the streets in Japan this narrow?"

"No, this is a very old neighborhood. The newer areas and main streets are much wider."

Further down the street, Sam noticed a small, inconspicuous opening between two buildings. The wooden entryway, surrounded by greenery like a garden arch, looked very old. "What's in there?"

"That's the community temple."

"Can anyone visit?"

"Yes. I'll take you there another time. I wanted to show you the park so you can bring Jack. The rest of the family doesn't come here often, but it's one of my favorite places."

Deceptively large, with a wide, wooded path, the park was unlike any Sam had ever seen. A dark pond with wooden platforms on each side sat near the front entrance. The platforms jutted over the water like miniature docks, and young boys squatted on them with fishing lines and buckets. "I'm not sure if there are any fish in there, but the children seem to enjoy playing in the water. Come. I want to show you something."

Past the pond, she veered off the wooded path and cut across a wide grassy clearing. She stopped at the far edge and climbed a long set of shallow steps to the top of a hill. At the top, she moved to the side so Sam could see.

"It's a slide," Sam exclaimed. "With rollers?"

Colorful metal rollers, almost small enough for Sam to wrap her hand around, lined the slide from top to bottom.

"They move. Try it out!"

Sam sat at the top of the slide and gave herself a push with her hands. She gathered speed as the rollers propelled her forward until she felt as if she was flying. At the bottom, the slide leveled out, and she slowed until she reached the end. Looking back, she saw Annie flying down the slide toward her and quickly moved out of the way. Annie had her arms in the air and let out a whoop.

"Best slide ever. I can't wait to show Jack."

"There are some little wooden shrines further down the path." Annie pointed in the opposite direction from the park entrance. "We should probably head back, though. I have to prepare for my classes. You can explore some more when you bring Jack."

Sam nodded. "Everything is so different here."

"I'm still learning things all the time. The language and culture are entwined in a way that allows many nuances to go unspoken. Sometimes, people say things to me, and although I understand the words, I completely miss the point. Luckily, Takashi is good at letting me know when I'm missing something."

"Everyone seems so kind and polite. Are they patient with you when you make a mistake?"

"Most people are very patient with visiting foreigners, assuming that you couldn't possibly understand their culture, even if they tried to explain it. But, when you marry into a Japanese family, your status changes. You are suddenly expected to toe the line. You're expected to understand all the rules that no one has explained to you. Even with Takashi's help, I've had trouble fitting in."

"I hope you'll explain some of them to me if you think of them. I know I'll never understand like you do, but I'm very interested."

"Sure. Let's start with your offer to help with the housework." Annie grinned. "I know you feel guilty being waited on, but it's a great source of pride for Oba. The harder she works and the more comfortable you are, the more esteemed she appears to family and neighbors."

Sam thought about that. "I think I understand. In this case, it's important for me to respect her wishes, even if it makes me feel like a burden."

"I'm afraid so."

"Is there anything else I should know right away?"

"Probably, but my mind's just gone blank." Annie laughed a large guffaw before she put her hand over her mouth and giggled. "My family and friends don't appreciate my natural boisterousness. I have to remember to tone it down."

"Nooo. Really?"

"I startle people, and they stare. Takashi just snickers, but I find it embarrassing."

They arrived back at the house, and Sam followed Annie inside, nearly colliding with her when she forgot to remove her shoes.

"Tadaima!" Annie called. "Would you like another cup of coffee before we go to the studio?"

"Yes!" Sam grinned. "How do you remember everything?"

"It becomes a habit, like putting on your seatbelt. By the time you go home, you'll probably be on automatic pilot."

Chapter 4

The Akiyama family business fascinated Jack. Takashi was a chef, while Jack's uncle, Junichi, took care of sales and the administrative side. Jack filled with questions as he observed production, but he didn't want to get in the way.

Takashi paused instructing his assistants and glanced over at Jack. "No questions?"

"So many, but you're very busy."

"I cook and talk. Many helpers." He waved his arm around at his staff and resumed chopping.

"Well, these lacquer boxes; aren't they expensive?"

"Yes. We deliver them today and return tomorrow."

"And how do you decide what to put in each compartment?"

"Every bento has rice, protein, and vegetable. We make two protein and two vegetable every day and add such nori, egg, ginger, and wasabi. Today, we have karaage and sashimi, broccoli, and gomae."

Jack looked at him questioningly. "I know what sashimi and broccoli are."

"Karaage is small fried chickens." He speared a bite-sized piece of chicken with a toothpick and handed it to Jack, who popped it in his mouth.

"Delicious. Popcorn chicken, but better."

"Gomae is spinach with sesame. Here. Try."

Jack accepted a small plate with wilted spinach on it and wrinkled his nose. Takashi handed him some chopsticks and waited for him to try it, so he took a bite. "It tastes way better than it looks. Almost like… peanut butter? I love it."

Takashi nodded happily. "Our food is good. That why we have many customers."

"Do they come here and pick them up?"

"No, we take." Looking behind Jack, he smiled and bowed. "Shima-san." He then burst into a long string of Japanese, which left Jack baffled. "Jyaku-kun, this is Shima-san. He live next house and sell us vegetables. I take you there later."

Bowing, Jack said, "Hajimemashite. Jack desu."

Mr. Shima, short and slender, with a scar above the right side of his lip, bowed as well. "Hajimemashite." He continued his discussion with Takashi before bowing again and taking his leave.

"He father's very good friend."

"Where *is* your father?"

"He go see new customer. Be soon here. I show how make bento." Picking up one of the beautiful black and red boxes, he showed Jack how to carefully place each food for maximum visual appeal, then let him practice making them for the family lunch.

Sam removed her shoes and followed Annie into the studio, glancing around in surprise. "Did you design this?"

"Yes, with input. Do you like it?"

"It's amazing." She tilted her head. "How did you make it look so clean and also somehow… comfortable?"

Annie joined her in surveying the room. The white table, tile floor, and cabinets were offset by a very light green paint and round carpet. The walls were bare, with the exception of a clock and a large whiteboard. "I think it's the simplicity. Check out the kids' classroom." She indicated a second room.

Sam stuck her head inside the room. "Wow. Just wow. Lucky kids." A thick, colorful carpet covered most of the floor, and charts hung on white walls, along with a whiteboard. Shelves overflowed with books and games.

"We sit on the floor and learn with songs and games.

"When the children graduate to middle school, we move into the adult classroom." Annie smiled. "I also have a small kitchenette and a toilet."

Hearing the pride in her voice, Sam grinned. "It's perfect. I almost want to be an English teacher so I can have one too."

Annie moved to the whiteboard and began writing questions. "Since you're here, we'll let the students practice on you. You don't mind, do you?"

"I guess not," Sam said dubiously.

⸻ ⸺❦⸺ ⸻

When the first student, Kazue Minami, arrived for her private lesson, Annie said, "Good morning, Kazue. I would like you to meet my friend Samantha."

Although five-foot-two in moderate heels, Kazue had presence. Dressed impeccably in a black skirt and jacket, Sam thought her very chic, and she smelled wonderful.

The three of them sat around the table, and Annie prompted Kazue to introduce herself and ask Sam the questions on the board.

Sitting with her back very straight and her lips pursed, Kazue looked down at the table. "My name is Kazue Minami. What is your name?"

"My name is Sam Olivares. Nice to meet you." Sam smiled.

"Why is your hair red?"

"Umm…"

"I want to know."

"I like this color."

"The school sent us home if we colored our hair or pierced our ears."

Sam nodded, unsure how to respond.

Glancing at the whiteboard, Kazue asked, "Where are you from?"

"I'm from New Mexico."

Kazue looked up. "Mexico?"

"No, New Mexico. It's in the United States, near Texas."

"Are you married?"

"Yes. My husband is a policeman."

"My husband owns a big company."

"Do you have children?"

"Yes, my son Akio works with his father."

"Does he live with you?"

"Yes." Kazue glanced at Annie, then at the whiteboard. "Do you have children?"

"Not yet."

"Why? You don't like children?"

Sam grinned. "I haven't been married very long."

"Is your husband tall like you?"

"Yes. We're about the same height."

"You will have big children. Akio-kun is taller than his father."

"You could be right." Sam nodded and noticed they had come to the end of Annie's questions. "What is that perfume you're wearing? It smells very nice."

"It's Channel N°5. I have worn it for many years."

"Sam's right. It really smells nice. Do you have any more questions for her?"

Kazue, looking down again, asked, "Do you live in Japan?"

"No, I'm just visiting."

"Did you meet Annie in Australia?"

Annie jumped in as Sam was considering her answer. "Sam came to Japan with her cousin, Jack, who is also Takashi's cousin."

"Yes, you told me about Jack." Kazue nodded.

"Your English is excellent, Kazue. How long have you been studying?" Sam asked.

"Since I was in school. Many years."

The students from the next class began to arrive, so Annie stood. "Great job, Kazue. I'll see you on Thursday."

After she left, Annie leaned toward Sam and whispered, "I'll tell you about her later."

The four students in the second class were chatty and filled with enthusiasm. It was obvious to Sam how much they liked Annie and each other. Unfortunately, their English was not as advanced, but they tried hard.

Annie had provided each of them with a basic textbook, which began with the verb 'to be,' and they each introduced themselves. Sam was surprised to see Jack's aunt in the class. Her bright eyes and gregarious interactions with her peers allowed Sam to see her in a different light.

Oba went first and introduced herself as Etsuko. Then, Annie asked the lively woman sitting next to her to take a turn.

"I am Izumi Shima. I live there." She waved toward the house next door with a rough, reddened hand. "I am fifty-three old. My daughter is Keiko. I sell vegetables."

"Very good. The Shima family owns the produce stand next door, Sam. How about Yoko?"

The student sitting next to Izumi was taller than her friends. She wore neat slacks and a colorful blouse, her hair in a French twist. Sam was distracted by a shiny coating on her face that looked something like Vaseline. "I am Yoko Murakami. I am forty-eight years old. I do not have children. I am a housewife." *Maybe it's some kind of moisturizer. She could pass for thirty.*

"That's great, Yoko. Now Asami."

"I am Asami Hirano. I am sixty. My son is died. I am cold." She hugged herself with arms as thin and frail as those of a China doll.

"Very good. Let me get you a blanket. Sam, would you introduce yourself? Simply please."

The four students gazed at her expectantly.

"My name is Samantha Olivares. You can call me Sam. I am twenty-six years old. I don't have any children yet. I am a rancher."

"What is rancher?" Izumi asked.

"I raise horses and cows. It's like a farm."

All of the women nodded and smiled. Annie returned and handed Asami a fuzzy blanket to put on her lap.

"Sam is a cowboy," Yoko happily announced.

Grinning, Annie said, "Cow*girl*, Yoko."

"Photos?" Izumi asked.

Sam held up a finger and scrolled through the gallery on her phone. "Here." She handed her phone to Izumi. "This is my horse, Ghost."

Eyes wide, all of the women admired the picture and began peppering Annie with questions in Japanese. The hour flew by, leaving Sam exhausted but feeling like she knew the four women a little better, especially Oba.

"Our class is finished for today, but Sam will be here next time, so we can ask her more about her ranch."

<hr>

Once the last of the students departed, Annie said, "You're a natural, Sam. I wish I could keep you."

"Your ladies are so much fun."

"They all have a story. The Minami family lives across the street, and they have a lot of money, so they are a little…"

"Snobby?"

"I guess. It's difficult to explain because they live in this neighborhood and have to act nice…noblesse oblige? They aren't well-liked, especially now that Kazue's husband is trying to get the beach rezoned for construction."

"Is that why she doesn't attend the group class?"

"Yes and no. The other ladies don't want her in their class, but she's also a much higher-level speaker and has the money for private lessons."

"Why do you call them by their first names?"

"I try to include culture in our language lessons, and part of that is getting them comfortable dropping honorifics. They don't have to include their ages, but since we are studying the use of the verb 'to be,' we have to keep it fairly simple. It also helps them learn numbers."

"Is Asami sick?"

"Yes." Annie frowned. "That's another reason everyone is unhappy with the Minami family. Yoshinori, Kazue's husband, recently laid off Asami's husband right when he really needs money for medical expenses. Japanese people don't usually talk about money, especially their own, but everyone is aware of the situation. There's a lot of resentment."

"Isn't there something we can do? At home, we would have a fundraiser to help someone in need."

"I don't know. Maybe. I'll ask Takashi what he thinks, but anything public would hurt their pride. Are you ready for lunch? The men usually bring us bento boxes at lunchtime."

Sam's stomach rumbled in response, making them laugh.

<hr>

The entire family gathered in the dining room for lunch.

"Itadakimasu," they intoned, lifting the lids from their bento boxes.

Jack had helped create them, so he knew what to expect, but when Sam lifted her lid, she gasped.

"It's beautiful," she said with reverence. "Like a work of art."

Takashi spoke rapidly with Annie, and she interpreted. "Takashi would like to know more about your perspective. How it appears to you, and why you like it. Could you describe your first impressions?"

Pausing, Sam considered. "Each type of food is a different shape and color, and the garnishes add even more variation. Opening the box is exciting. I don't know what everything will taste like, but the presentation is beautiful, and it smells delicious."

"I think he'd also like to hear what you think about the combination of flavors and textures, but please go ahead and eat; then we can talk about it." Annie smiled and took a bite.

"Could I have a fork, please?"

"Sorry!" Annie popped up and hurried into the kitchen.

When Sam finished her meal and set down her fork, Takashi looked at her expectantly. She realized that the entire family was watching her, and she blushed. "I don't know much about Japanese food, so I'm probably not the best person to ask."

"Nonsense. You are the best person to ask because you don't have a lot of preconceived ideas."

"Well, I enjoyed the different flavor profiles, and I felt like the rice was a good palette cleanser in between. It went well with everything. The chicken was moist on the inside and crunchy on the outside, not overly salty, and delicious with some lemon squeezed on top. I haven't had raw fish before, but that sashimi was soft and buttery, and the soy sauce and wasabi gave it a kick."

"Is kick a good thing?" Takashi asked.

"I think so," Jack offered. "Like a little 'wow'."

Takashi smiled.

"Then the vegetables. The broccoli was simple but not overcooked, so it added a fresh crunch. That other one was kind of sweet. Very tasty. Altogether, I got five different flavors and textures. That made the meal very satisfying."

Annie was busy interpreting, so it took a moment for the rest of the family to react. They all smiled, and Takashi asked Jack, "Do you agree?"

"Yes. Everything was great quality, tasty, and fresh."

"I have told him so myself, but he thinks I'm just being nice. He always wants to know what foreigners truly think about his food. He has a dream of expanding, translating the menu into English, and creating an app that anyone can order from, not just businesses. His father isn't quite on board, but he'll come around."

"My friend Akio, he can make app."

Oji frowned at the mention of Takashi's friend, and Sam tried to remember where she'd heard that name.

"Kazue's son," Annie whispered.

Realization dawned. *Oji doesn't like the Minami family.*

At Jack's questioning look, Sam mumbled, "Later."

Chapter 5

After lunch, Sam and Jack followed Annie outside. "Would you like to go to the supermarket with me? We have small grocery, meat, and produce shops around here, but I usually make a trip to a larger store about once a week. It saves time, and there's greater selection. Maybe next week I can take you to Nagoya. That's where I can buy a lot of imported food. It's expensive, but sometimes I get cravings."

"I'd love to go. How about you, cuz?"

"Sure. I can't even imagine what we'll find. We have a few Asian grocery stores in Albuquerque, but not an honest-to-goodness Japanese supermarket."

"Imagine my complete ignorance. I've never seen any kind of Asian market; I'm lucky if the supermarket in Las Rodillas carries soy sauce."

"If you want, I can teach you how to make a couple dishes when Etsuko isn't looking." Annie grinned. "Or Takashi can probably teach you a thing or two while he's working."

"That would be so fun, don't you think so?" He didn't answer. "Jack?" Sam looked in the direction he was staring and saw Oji arguing with a man who looked about his same age and stature. "Who's that?"

Annie's lips pursed, and her eyebrows drew together. "That's Yoshinori Minami, Kazue's husband. Worse, Takashi's headed over there to get in the middle of it."

"Do you need to go talk to him?"

"No, he wouldn't appreciate that."

Jack had to get involved, of course. He strode purposely over to the small group of men. "What's going on?"

The men gazed up at him in silence.

Finally, Takashi said, "This is family talk, Jack. Not for you."

Feeling as if he'd been struck, Jack took a step back, then turned and walked away. He walked past Sam and Annie and into the house, leaving his shoes willy-nilly in the entrance. Entering their room, he closed the sliding doors and pulled out his suitcase. Throwing everything inside, he was just closing it when Sam joined him.

"What happened? This looks drastic."

"Takashi just told me I'm not family. I don't want to be here anymore."

"I'm sure that's not exactly what he said. Do you mean you don't want to be in Japan anymore, or you just don't want to be staying in this house?"

"I don't know. I'm upset."

"Well, let's just go out for a while. Maybe Annie can give us a ride to the train station."

"I don't want anything from them."

"We don't know how to call a cab or how to walk there."

Jack pulled out his phone and opened the GPS app, drawing a rough map on a piece of paper. "Let's go," he said gruffly.

Sam followed him as he stomped out of the house and past Annie, standing alone in the drive.

"Hey. What's going on? Where are you going?" she jogged to keep up with them.

"I don't know, exactly, Hamamatsu, I think. Jack's feeling offended. You might want to ask Takashi what he said. We're just going on a little outing. Hopefully, we'll be back tonight... maybe tomorrow."

Looking back, Sam saw Annie had stopped and was watching them walk away. *It must be hard for her sometimes.*

"Jack. Please slow down. I know you're disappointed, but I can't keep up."

"I didn't make you come."

Sam stopped. "Would you rather I didn't?"

Jack stopped, too, and turned to face her. "No, I need you with me."

"Okay, I'm here. Please be nice."

He hugged her. "I'm sorry. I shouldn't take it out on you. Let's go find something fun to do."

Sam and Jack disembarked in Hamamatsu. "It's like taking a train from Santo Milagro to Las Rodillas. No… even better. To Albuquerque."

Jack glanced around. "We should have looked up where to go once we got here."

"Don't worry. I did already, while we were on the train. I made some notes on my phone, and there's a tourist information center in the station. I bet we can get a map."

Jack lifted one eyebrow. "What would I ever do without you? I've never met anyone who's so prepared all the time."

Sam gave a little snort and nodded toward a sign in English with an arrow. "We could get very lost if we're not careful."

The information center, once they found it, was very clean and colorful. The two women working at the counter were friendly, and by the time they left, with recommendations for a hotel and restaurant and a map, Jack's shoulders had lost some of their tension. "Let's get checked into the hotel, then maybe we can do some sightseeing."

"I'd like to see the castle. That lady said we could take the bus from here."

"Okay. The hotel's only a three-minute walk. It shouldn't take long to get a room."

As they walked, Jack's senses reeled. Music and voices, fragrant aromas, signs he couldn't read, and so many people. He saw the hotel from a distance. With fourteen floors, it was difficult to miss.

"There it is," he said, pointing.

"I think I might have whiplash. It's really hard to take in everything at once."

"True. I didn't realize the time. We'll need to buy a few things since we didn't bring our luggage, and it's almost dinner time. Do you want to save the castle for tomorrow?"

"Yeah, we don't want to have to rush."

<hr>

Jack held the door open for Sam, who stopped and gaped at the immense lobby. Glistening tiles, enormous chandeliers, a piano, and escalators, everything in warm gold and cream colors, providing a feeling of luxury and elegance.

"Impressive," Jack said. "I wonder how much they charge for their rooms."

"I know, right?"

As they neared the reception counter, the young female clerk scurried into the back room, replaced momentarily by a mild-looking man with round spectacles. "How may I be of service?" he asked politely.

"We'd like a room for two nights," Jack said, glancing at Sam for confirmation.

She gave an almost imperceptible nod, and the man at the desk produced what looked like a menu but was actually a booklet with pictures and descriptions of each room with prices for one, two, or more guests.

The first room was a beautiful suite with a living room and a dining room, which cost over ninety-six thousand yen.

"How much is that in dollars? Ninety?"

Jack frowned. "No, I think that's around six-fifty. Isn't it?" He looked at the man behind the counter.

"Yes, sir. The most affordable is the twin room."

"We'll take that one." It was about one hundred and seventy dollars, certainly more reasonable.

"Isn't that a lot?" Sam asked on their way upstairs.

"We could have stayed in a lower-end hotel for considerably less, but we might as well enjoy ourselves while we're here, don't you think?"

"Yes, I suppose so."

Jack opened the door to their room and stepped inside. "After the grandeur downstairs, the room's a little disappointing."

"It's a room." Sam shrugged. "It'll be fine. Everything exciting is outside." She grinned and ran to the window. "I can't wait to get back out there. Let's go look around."

<hr>

Wandering around downtown Hamamatsu was exhilarating. They walked in and out of small shops, leaving the large department stores for another time. The first time they entered a shop, Sam flinched in surprise when the two employees called out, "Irasshaimase!" But by the third shop, she figured out that it must be some kind of greeting. "Do you know what they're saying?"

"No, but they all say it, so it must be something like 'Welcome,' I guess."

"Do we have everything we need now? I'm getting hungry."

"Yes, and that restaurant they recommended is just around the corner."

Ducking under a flapping canvas banner and sliding open the wooden door, they were once again greeted with 'Irasshaimase'.

Sam hardly noticed because her nose was assailed by such wonderful smells that she drooled a little. "Cuz, this smells like heaven."

They took a seat at a small square table and accepted menus from the waitress. She was a round, matronly-looking woman with her hair pulled severely from her face. Smiling, she said something in Japanese and waited for a response.

Sam looked at Jack, who shrugged.

"Biiru kudasai," he said.

"Hai," she replied before turning and heading toward the counter.

"What did she say?"

"No idea."

"What did you say?"

"I asked for beer. That seemed like a safe answer."

"She didn't ask what kind. I wonder what we'll get."

"Does it matter?" Jack laughed. "Let's see if we can figure out the menu."

They were both pleasantly surprised when they opened their menus and found pictures.

"This makes it much easier," Sam said. She glanced around at the other patrons. "I think these are all very small plates, so we can order lots of different ones. These look good." She pointed at chicken skewers. "And this… and this. How will we ever choose? I want everything."

When the waitress returned with two large bottles of Asahi Super-Dry and two small glasses, she again asked them something in Japanese, and Jack pointed out eight items on the menu. She noted his choices on a small pad of paper and left the table. "Our first night here, I learned that when you're drinking beer like this, you refill each other's glasses whenever they're empty." Jack picked up one of the bottles and poured beer into Sam's glass and then his own.

"Well, that's good to know." She picked up her glass. "Cheers."

"Kampai."

They each took a sip and agreed that the beer was delicious.

"I hope the food gets here soon."

"You're in luck. Here she comes." Jack smiled as the server began setting small plates on their table.

Examining the food on each plate, Sam gave each one a sniff before she took a bite. "I like this one." She pointed to a plate of shredded carrot and burdock garnished with sesame seeds. "It's a little sweet and savory."

Jack took a bite, chewing thoughtfully. "Crunchy, but not hard. I like it, too. And these asparagus wrapped in bacon." He picked up one. "I don't even like asparagus, but these are delicious."

"Bacon makes everything better."

They worked their way through rice balls grilled in soy sauce, chicken skewers, and shredded salad.

"I know what this is. We had it in our bento box at lunch."

"Gomae." Jack nodded. "One of my favorites so far. Who knew spinach could taste so good?"

Sam refilled his glass. "Are you ready to talk about what happened?"

"I don't know. Did I overreact?"

"Maybe. Takashi's English isn't perfect. He might not have realized how you would take what he said."

Jack looked thoughtful as he chewed. "My father constantly rejected me, so telling me I'm not really family hit me hard."

"Do they know how your father treated you?"

Jack shook his head.

"I think Takashi probably meant that the argument was between neighbors. Annie told me that Mr. Minami is trying to get the beach-front property rezoned."

Slumping, Jack drank his beer and refilled their glasses. "It was such a knee-jerk reaction. I don't want to be some random foreign guest. I need family."

"I guess you don't consider me family anymore, but you're all I've got," Sam mumbled.

"You have Tom and his family now."

"That's not the same."

"It's about the same as my Japanese family. I don't know them at all. You're still my only real family, blood-related or not." He put his hand on hers and smiled.

"Thanks, cuz," she whispered, swiping away a stray tear.

After Sam and Jack left, Annie went to her studio, sat at the table, and put her head in her hands. Big, fat tears rolled down her face. *He always has to ruin everything. I finally make a friend and he has to chase her away.* She pulled out her notebook and a pen and began to write.

Looking up when Takashi entered the studio, she noticed the sun had set. Her stomach rumbled.

"You missed dinner," he said gently, handing her a plate. "You're writing poetry. What's wrong?"

"What did you say to Jack?"

"Nothing. What do you mean?"

"He got very upset and left with Sam. I don't know where they went or when they'll be back."

"He's not *your* cousin. Why do you care?"

Annie frowned at him. "I care because I don't have many friends, and you just chased away my new one."

"You're angry with me."

"Yes! I'm angry. And you'd better fix it. What did you say?"

"He tried to interfere in father's argument, and I told him it was a family matter."

"So basically, you told him he's not family."

"No." Takashi shook his head.

"Augh! Go away."

"Annie…"

"Leave. I don't want to talk to you right now." She felt a twinge of guilt as she watched him slouch away but then felt her anger well up again. *Stupid… selfish… clueless.* Poisoned by her resentment, she felt ugly inside.

Chapter 6

The day after Sam and Jack left, Annie began to panic. She imagined them wandering around Hamamatsu, lost and unable to communicate. The rest of the family seemed unconcerned, which she found frustrating. Although it was a long shot, she decided to look for them. *They're on foot, so maybe they've stayed close to the train station.*

Surmising that Etsuko would think she was nuts, she didn't bother telling anyone where she was going. She left a note on the kitchen counter so they wouldn't worry.

When she arrived in Hamamatsu, she began to realize how difficult it might be to locate them. Scanning the sea of humanity rushing through the lobby, she spotted a sign that read 'Information Center'. *Would they have gone there? I didn't even know it existed. It's worth a try.*

She followed the signs and entered the office. One of the women behind the counter shook her head when Annie began to describe Sam and Jack, but the other, who was helping a German visitor, looked over and asked her to wait.

After she finished helping her customer, she approached Annie. "I saw your friends yesterday. I recommended a hotel near here, but I don't know if they went there."

Annie thanked the woman profusely and headed for the hotel. It wasn't far, and when she entered the lobby, she stopped and gaped at the opulence. *I shouldn't be surprised. Of course, they recommended the poshest one.* She approached the reception desk, and the clerk on duty sprinted into the back, replaced almost immediately by a solemn-looking young man.

He seemed surprised that she spoke Japanese, and, although he insisted he could not give out guest information, he suggested that she might like to rest and gave a slight nod in the direction of a sofa facing the main entry.

Thus, Annie was sitting on the sofa when Sam and Jack returned. She stood abruptly and rushed to join them, throwing her arms around Sam. "I'm so glad you're okay. I've been worried."

Sam's eyebrows rose. "I'm sorry, Annie. I didn't have your number to let you know we were staying over. Would you like to join us for lunch?"

"That sounds lovely. Are you okay, Jack?"

"Yes. Sam talked me off the ledge." He grinned.

"Will you come back with me this afternoon?"

"Aww, I didn't get to see the Botanical Gardens yet."

"We reserved one more night at the hotel, but you can stay with us if you'd like."

"Right-o. Even better. What have you seen so far?"

"Yesterday, we bought some sundries and ate at a cute little restaurant with lots of tiny plates of food. I want to eat there again."

"That's probably an izakaya, a Japanese-style pub. I love them, too."

"Then today, I drug Jack to Hamamatsu Castle."

"That's pretty far, isn't it?"

"We took the blue bus."

"You two are very resourceful. I'm impressed. There's an excellent ramen shop near here. I'll take you there, then we can go see the flower park."

"What do you think, cuz?"

"Sounds good to me."

⸻ ⟡ ⸻

Jack followed Annie and Sam to the ramen shop, feeling somewhat relieved that she would be returning with them.

He felt awkward about their abrupt departure and what he would say when they returned.

Entering a tiny shop consisting of nothing but a long counter and a row of stools in front of a narrow cooking space, Annie said, "This is my favorite ramen place."

"Do they have menus?"

"Not really. There are three basic kinds of soup base: soy sauce, miso, or salt, and you can choose the toppings you want. The garnishes are on the counter. I like the soy base with pork. Then, I add sesame seeds and green onions on top."

"I'll just have whatever you have."

"Me, too," Jack said. "And maybe some of that super dry beer. Do they have that?"

"It's very popular. I think you can find it almost anywhere, even in the vending machines."

"Whaaat? Beer in vending machines? Awesome idea!"

"If you get desperate, you can even buy hot coffee in a can."

"Are you hearing this, Jack? We need vending machines with beer and coffee."

Jack chuckled. "That's *all* you need."

Annie placed their orders. "This is a quick-in, quick-out place, so it'll be up in just a minute."

Jack wasn't sure which was more interesting, watching the owner of the shop put noodles from the cooking basket into a giant bowl, ladling soup, and adding toppings or watching Sam deal with the toppings.

She sniffed each one, poked it with a chopstick, took a nibble, then either popped it in her mouth with a smile or discarded it with a frown. So far, she had eaten the hardboiled egg and strips of pork, discarding the seaweed and the fish cake.

The soup was delicious, and as Jack noisily slurped the noodles with his chopsticks like everyone else, Sam carefully piled small amounts of noodles in her Chinese-style soup spoon, eating each small portion with the soup.

When they were finished, he and Annie had bowls full of broth, and Sam had a bowl full of noodles.

"Aren't you going to eat your noodles?" Annie asked.

"I don't have any more soup."

Jack chuckled. "Do you want more broth?"

"No, I'm pretty full."

"You'll be hungry tonight."

"Can we go back to the place we went last night?"

"Sure. Why not?"

<hr>

After lunch, Annie took them on the bus to the botanical gardens on the edge of Lake Hamana. The flowers were in full bloom, enchanting Sam. "These are my favorite," she said every time she saw a new type of flower. The long trellis covered in purple flowers was the most beautiful thing she had ever seen.

They strolled through the gardens and the greenhouse dubbed the 'Crystal Palace,' then took a guided tour on the 'Flower Train' to give their feet a rest.

"One more destination," Annie announced, as she led them back to the bus stop. "It's only four more stops."

Disembarking at the Hamanako Pal Pal stop, Sam's eyes widened. "Are we going to an amusement park?"

"No, we can do that another day if you like, but there's a ropeway that goes from here to the top of Mount Okusa and I thought you might like to see the view."

Sam and Jack were both glued to the window of the aerial tram as they ascended over the lake and after they had looked through the museum at the summit, they climbed to the observation deck on the roof, where they could see all the way to the Pacific Ocean.

The sun began to set, reflecting the vibrant pink and orange of the sky, and Sam sighed dreamily. "So beautiful."

"This is one of my favorite places," Annie agreed. "Takashi brought me here on our first date."

"Is everything okay?"

"Is it that obvious?"

"No, you just looked a little sad."

"Maybe we can talk about it later." She glanced at Jack. "It's kind of hard to explain. Why don't we head back now? I'm getting hungry."

<hr>

By the time they got back to downtown Hamamatsu, it was well past dinner time, and Jack's stomach was complaining. They ordered more than they needed at the izakaya but enjoyed Annie's input. Finding out the names of their favorite dishes and trying new ones elevated dinner's fun factor.

Sam found out the crunchy vegetable she liked so much was called kinpira gobo, and Annie explained the different types of yakitori. The skewered chicken came in different flavors, and one style was made entirely of skin.

"Hamamatsu is famous for gyouza, so we have to get some of that, too," she explained.

"What's that?"

"Pot stickers."

Sam looked at her questioningly.

"Like little fried pies with meat and cabbage in them. They're delicious. Have you had them before, Jack?"

"Yes. There are a few Japanese restaurants in Albuquerque."

By the time the server brought their food, they had filled and refilled each other's glasses several times, and Annie became more talkative. She talked about arriving in Japan from Australia eight years prior and falling in love with Takashi.

"It was like a dream. Everyone was so nice, and I loved everything about Japan, about teaching. Takashi was my first real boyfriend, and I couldn't imagine life without him. His family wasn't too sure about me since I'm a foreigner, but they accepted me for his sake."

"So, what's wrong?" Sam refilled her glass again and ate some yakitori.

"Lately, I've been feeling lonely and resentful. I don't see Takashi much, and I don't have many English-speaking friends. When you guys left, I was mad at him."

"Have you tried talking to him about how you feel?" Sam asked.

"I don't know how. We can't move to Australia because Takashi is expected to take over the bento business. We can't even move into our own place. His family has been talking about children, and I feel trapped. I know staying here and marrying him was my own choice, but I didn't consider the obligations I was taking on."

"Do you still love him?"

Annie nodded.

"Do you still love Japan?"

"Some things, I guess. Not as much as I did." She poured more beer into each glass. "Sometimes, I feel so old."

"How old are you?" Jack asked.

"Twenty-six, but it seems like all my choices have been taken away. I will live in that house until the day I die. No job shift, no travel, nothing interesting to look forward to. I'm afraid I'll turn into Takashi's mom."

"Oji's still relatively young. Maybe you could convince Takashi to move to Australia for a little while to learn new cooking techniques or business models. That would give the two of you a chance to refresh and reconnect," Sam suggested.

Annie's face brightened. "Do you think he would agree?"

"I don't know him well enough to say, but if he understands how unhappy you are, he might at least consider it."

Jack filled their glasses with the last of the beer and patted his flat stomach. "Do we want another bottle, or should we head back to the hotel?"

Looking at her watch, Annie said, "It's ten o'clock. I'm okay either way."

"Let's get back, then. I'm wrecked." Sam stood and placed her hands on the small of her back, stretching.

"Sam's still waking before dawn."

"Maybe we can buy a couple of beers from a vending machine." She grinned mischievously.

Chapter 7

Annie had classes scheduled for the next morning, so they returned to Iwata at seven. She rushed upstairs to get ready for her day, leaving Sam and Jack to their own devices. The house was shuttered and still.

"Maybe we should go for a walk," Jack suggested.

"Annie showed me a cool park the other day. You should see it."

"Lead the way."

Tiptoeing back outside and quietly closing the door, Jack followed Sam through the labyrinth of narrow streets. Here and there, shopkeepers were arranging their wares on the sidewalk in front of their stores.

"Is it much farther?"

"No, we're almost there."

The street dead-ended, and Sam turned left onto a wooded path. She pointed out the fishing hole and led Jack to the roller slide.

When he stepped onto the platform at the top, he looked down and laughed. "This is crazy. How does it work?"

"Watch this!" Sam sat on the rollers and gave herself a push. Faster and faster, she flew, throwing her arms in the air and shouting with glee.

Jack mimicked Sam's actions, his heart pounding as he picked up speed. *I hope Sam moves so we don't crash.* He found a measure of relief when the slide flattened, and he began to slow. "I was wondering how I was going to stop."

Flushed and grinning, Sam bent over with her hands on her knees. "Isn't it exhilarating? Let's do it again."

Jack laughed and followed her to the top again. Flying downward for the second time, he realized how alive he felt when he was with Sam. Whether riding horses on her ranch or trying new food, she was always so enthusiastic about everything she did, making everything an adventure. *I've missed her so much.*

<hr>

Sam stood at the base of the slide and watched Jack whoop as he flew toward her. *He is so beautiful,* she thought, admiring his tall, muscular frame in jeans and a button-down shirt. *He just lights up when he's happy; he deserves to be happy more often.*

Laughing as he climbed off the slide, he approached and said, "Thank you for being here with me. It wouldn't have been the same without you."

"I wouldn't have missed it. Come now, there's something else we have to see. Annie said there are some wooden shrines at the end of the path."

Walking back to the path, Sam strained her eyes to see their destination but saw only rocks and trees. She stopped abruptly, pointing. "What's that?"

He stopped as well, then dashed forward.

Breathing hard, they stopped a few feet from the man who lay prone on the path. Jack scanned the ground before approaching and checking for a pulse. "Sam, I need you to run back to the house and get someone to call the police."

"Is he dead?"

"Yes, and it looks like murder."

"Be right back."

Sam wasn't a runner, but she was athletic. She sprinted all the way to the Akiyama home and then stood gasping in the entryway. "Annie! I need your help." She didn't have time for protocol and didn't know what it would be in any case. "Annie!"

Annie hurried downstairs in her robe, a concerned look on her face.

"Could you call the police? We found a dead body in the park, and Jack says it looks like murder."

"Did you run all the way here?"

"Yes, please hurry. Jack is there by himself."

"I'll call, then throw some clothes on. Do you want a ride back?"

"No, I'll run. Could I get a glass of water?"

Sam took two gulps of water and ran back toward the park. When she got there, Jack had moved away from the body but was still scanning the area. "Have you discovered anything?"

"Yes. Here come the police. I wonder if they speak English." His brow furrowed, he reached into his pocket and pulled out a business card. "I had these translated just in case."

Sam felt a frisson of fear as two men in jumpsuits approached, followed by three uniformed police officers. *They look so serious. And suspicious. Do they think we did it?*

The one who seemed to be in charge spoke English. "Someone reported a death. Do you know this man?"

"No, sir. We were taking a walk and found him," Jack answered.

"Do you live near here?"

"I'm visiting family, the Akiyamas. Here is my card." He held out a business card and bowed low. "Yoroshiku onegaishimasu."

The policeman accepted Jack's card and inspected it. "I am Keibu Ito, Chief Inspector. You have no jurisdiction here, but I am happy to receive any information you have gathered."

"I think this man might be a neighbor, but when I saw him a couple of days ago, he had hair on his scalp. Maybe it wasn't the same man." He shook his head. "The body was warm when we found him, so death was recent."

"Did you see anyone else?"

"No."

"What was the cause of death?"

"The presence of petechiae, swollen lips, and the scarf around his neck could indicate that he was killed by strangulation, but I would recommend an autopsy."

"Of course you would." Keibu Ito studied Jack's card and chuckled, causing Jack to stiffen. "What is petechiae?"

"These small red dots behind his ear. May I move the scarf?"

"Yes, please."

Jack carefully moved the scarf and pointed out faint redness on the victim's neck. "My concerns are twofold. First, if this is the same man I saw two days ago, his sudden hair loss is concerning, possibly toxic alopecia."

"Toxic alopecia?"

"Hair loss, which could be caused by a number of illnesses, excessive vitamin A, or even poison. Also, I am not seeing the normal signs of self-defense. When someone is strangled, they panic. They fight with every ounce of strength they have, often injuring themselves in the process."

Inspector Ito gazed at the victim. "So, what are you suggesting?"

"I don't like to answer that question without opening him up, but it's possible that he died from something other than strangulation. If he's cremated, it will be too late. I would be glad to assist if I'm needed."

Ito frowned. "So, he might have been strangled or poisoned? Is there any chance he died a natural death? A heart attack, perhaps?"

"I don't know anything about his medical history, but I suppose it's possible. If this was *my* case, I'd have the crime scene technicians search the area for a cup or bottle, and if they find anything, check it for fingerprints and test the contents. Then, I'd order an autopsy."

Ito stiffened. "We are perfectly capable of investigating a crime scene, Dr. Olivares."

"Of course. I'm sorry if I offended you."

Ito gave him a brief nod.

Sam saw Annie approaching from the road and waved.

The uniformed policemen tried to prevent her from approaching, but Jack explained her presence to Inspector Ito, who ordered them to let her through.

"Akiyama Annie desu," Annie began.

"He speaks perfect English," Sam said.

"That makes everything easier, doesn't it?"

Ito kept his face neutral but pinkened slightly. "I went to college in Texas. Sometimes speaking English is very helpful."

Annie glanced at the body and gasped before looking away.

"Do you know this man?" Ito asked sharply.

"Yes. Minami-san lives—lived across the street from us."

One of the other officers approached. "Keibu Ito, kyuukyuusha kimashita."

Ito looked at Jack. "The ambulance is here. Do you think we can move the body?"

"Where are your crime scene technicians?"

"Our team does all of the investigating."

"I took pictures with my phone, but don't you have an official photographer?"

"We do; he is occupied elsewhere. May I see your photos?"

Jack handed him his phone and watched as Inspector Ito scrolled through the gallery. "Very professional. These will do."

"Did you notice he's grasping something in his right hand?"

Ito leaned forward to look. "What is it?"

"I don't know, but I took a photo. I recommend you bag it so it doesn't get lost, and do some testing to see what it is and if there are any fingerprints on it other than the victim's."

Looking offended once again, Ito said, "Of course."

Jack nodded. "Is there anything further I can assist you with?"

"No, we'll take it from here. But please send me those photos." He handed Jack his business card.

"Let's turn him over and get a few of the neck before they move him." Jack squatted next to the body and had Ito hold the scarf away from the neck as he took more pictures. Then he stood.

"You know where to find me, I think." He turned away to join Sam and Annie, who had parked her car on the street. "Was that the man arguing with Takashi and Oji day before yesterday?"

"Minami-san? Yes."

"Didn't he have hair?"

"Yes. Why?"

"He doesn't now."

"Maybe he shaved it?"

Jack slowly shook his head. "I don't think so."

Takashi jogged up the drive behind them when they got back to the house. "Did you just return?"

"No, we got back at seven."

"What is going on?"

Annie looked at Jack.

"Sam and I found a body in the park."

Takashi looked stunned. "Is that joke?"

"It was Minami-san," Annie said.

"Did he heart attack?"

"It looks like murder," Sam said.

"Aren't you some kind of police?" Takashi looked at Jack with a frown.

"No, I'm a forensic medical examiner."

"What is that?"

"A doctor who investigates unexpected deaths," Sam said.

Takashi's face was blank when he said, "M. Where they now?"

"Who?"

"Police."

Jack shrugged.

"We go tell family."

Jack and Sam trailed after Takashi and Annie and stood in the doorway observing the family.

Having assumed that careful observation would give him a solid idea of their thoughts and feelings, Jack quickly realized his mistake. Not only did his family members keep their faces almost entirely immobile, but their voices did not reflect their sentiments either. Without understanding their words, he was unable to decipher their emotional responses. *This scene would look very different at home.*

He glanced at Sam and made a slight nod toward their guest room, then backed out of the living room and turned. Quietly sliding the doors open, he waited for Sam to follow and closed them again. Their room, with its paper doors, was not soundproof, so Jack whispered, "Could you get any reading on their reactions?"

"Not really," she whispered back. "Your grandparents had no reaction; like someone had just said rain was forecast for next week. Your aunt and uncle commented, but without knowing what they said, I can't even guess. How do they even do that?"

"Do what?"

"Keep their faces from showing anything."

They both looked toward the doors to their room at the sound of a light knock. Sam rose to open them and found Annie standing there.

"Can I come in?" she whispered.

"Of course." Sam moved out of the way.

"Breakfast will be ready in a few minutes. Takashi and his father had to get to work."

"Didn't you have classes this morning?"

Annie looked at Sam. "My first class is Mrs. Minami. I don't think she'll come today."

"What made you gasp when you saw Minami-san in the park?"

Annie fidgeted under Jack's piercing gaze. "I was just surprised that he was the victim."

"No, I think it was something else. What did you see?"

Glancing at the doors and then at her hands, she finally settled her focus on Jack's face. "You're family, just like I am. I don't want to cause any trouble, and what I saw will cause trouble."

Still watching her, Jack remained still.

"The scarf. It belongs to Takashi's mother." Her shoulders slumped. "Of course, there's no way she was in the park strangling someone this morning."

"Why do you think someone used her scarf?"

"That's what worries me the most. How would anyone even get it unless she accidentally left it somewhere? No one in the family would use it because it would point right at her."

"They might if they knew she had an unbreakable alibi," Sam mumbled.

"That would be quite a gamble."

"I'm so worried." Annie wrung her hands.

"What did Oji and Oba say when Takashi told them about the murder?"

"His mother said, 'Poor Akio.' That's his son's name. And his father said, 'Better for everyone'."

"What about his wife?" Sam asked.

Annie sighed. "She hated him."

"Gohan," called Oba from the kitchen.

Chapter 8

At breakfast the next morning, Annie brought Sam's coffee to the table. "I know it's Friday, but next week is Golden Week, and I canceled classes yesterday, so I've scheduled the ladies' group class this morning. Would you like to come?"

Sam glanced at Jack, who winked at her. "Absolutely. I wouldn't miss it."

"Would you like to come too, Jack?"

"Thank you, but Takashi asked me if I'd like to learn how to make gyouza this morning."

"Oh, yes! Learn how to make them. We'll need to have that when we get home."

Annie laughed. "What about yakitori?"

"Oh, yeah. You'd better spend all your time in that kitchen and write everything down."

"Yes, ma'am." He saluted.

※

After toast and coffee, Sam followed Annie to her studio and helped her set up for her class. She was thinking about the murder when Annie interrupted her thoughts.

"Jack is really handsome, isn't he?"

"So intelligent, too. He got lucky in the gene department."

"Were your dads really tall?"

Sam glanced at her. *Didn't they tell her about Jack's dad? I guess he must have been tall. I wonder if Jack wants to find him.* "Yes, practically giants." She grinned.

Blushing, Annie apologized. "I guess that didn't come out quite right."

"Don't worry. I do feel a little bit like a giant here."

The students began to arrive and took their places around the table. They whispered amongst themselves until Annie walked to the head of the table.

"Good morning. Thank you for coming today. I know you all heard about Mr. Minami." Annie cupped her hand around her ear. "Let's try to talk about it in English. Eigo de hanashimashou."

Trying to stem the flow of gossip was useless, so Annie did her best to translate for Sam and teach the ladies useful phrases in the process. Sam, on the other hand, didn't want to inadvertently divulge information that the police wanted to keep under wraps.

"Yoko wants to know how you found the body."

"Jack and I were taking a walk in the park."

"How did he die?" Annie translated for Asami.

"I don't think the police have made an official determination." Sam glanced at Annie for help. *That's not something I can comment on before it's official.*

Conversation continued to swirl around her, some of which she understood and some she didn't. The women contemplated who might want Mr. Minami dead and debated whether it was one of their neighbors or an unknown stranger from the city.

Jack had spent the morning with Takashi, making gyouza, Sam's most recent favorite food. They weren't difficult to make, but time-consuming. A teaspoon full of delicious pork and cabbage mixture was placed in the center of a thin, round skin and then folded into a small dumpling. No matter how hard he tried, however, his was never as perfect as Takashi's. He pan-fried and then steamed the dumplings, and his efforts were presented to the family for lunch. Although imperfect, they were delicious and received rave reviews.

"The secret is in the dipping sauce," Annie said. "It's half soy sauce, half vinegar, and a splash of hot sesame oil."

"I like more vinegar," Takashi said.

"So good," Sam mumbled around a mouthful.

After lunch, Jack received a phone call and excused himself. "I'll be back soon. Thank you for the cooking lesson, Takashi."

Inspector Ito was sitting in a dark corner of the local izakaya, facing the entrance, when Jack arrived. There weren't many patrons due to the early hour, and although Ito was wearing an ill-fitting suit and his hair looked like it hadn't been combed, he was unable to disguise his profession. *I wonder what it is. His watchfulness?* Jack pulled out a chair and joined him at the table.

Pouring beer into a fresh glass, Ito said, "Thank you for joining me. Most people call me by my title, but you can call me Minoru when it's just the two of us."

Jack picked up his glass. "Kampai." He raised it in appreciation. "Have you eaten?"

"I asked the server to bring a few things when you got here. I spoke to my superior this morning and asked him if you could attend the autopsy."

Jack raised an eyebrow.

Minoru stared into his glass. "In some ways, my foreign studies made my life more difficult. I can see that you are very good at your job, and I want your input, but my superior..." He took a sip of his beer and paused as the server brought their food.

When she left, he began again. "The kitchen sink in my mother's house faces away from the window. From the sink, she can see into the dining area. I asked her once if she wouldn't rather have her workspace face the window so she could see outdoors, and I told her about American-style kitchens." Pouring more beer into Jack's glass, he looked into his eyes. "She told me that looking outside and daydreaming leads to laziness. She would rather focus on her task and watch the family to make sure they had everything they needed."

Jack wondered where Minoru was heading with his story.

"In Japan, most people share similar beliefs, and some of those beliefs have become so ingrained that they have become part of our language and culture."

Jack studied Minoru's face with his fathomless black eyes, trying to unravel the meaning behind his words.

Picking up a skewer of yakitori, Minoru said, "Itadakimasu," and took a bite.

Jack did the same and poured more beer into Minoru's glass.

"Although Japanese people might be polite, I think we feel a kind of superiority about the way we work together to accomplish our goals and our ability to understand each other on a deep level. These things are difficult to explain, and no one ever really tries."

"So..." Jack began slowly. "Your chief is kind of biased, like your mom with her kitchen? He thinks that your system is best and that I might introduce unwelcome procedures?"

His eyes widened slightly; Minoru nodded. "Yes, I think that's it." He lowered his head. "I'm afraid that we might get the same reaction from everyone, including the professor who usually performs autopsies."

Jack sipped his beer and nodded thoughtfully.

"I can't openly defy my superior's orders, but I would still like your input. Perhaps we can meet for beer again."

Jack smiled his understanding. "I would like that very much. You might enjoy getting to know my cousin Sam as well. She's very smart."

"I don't know. Is she the very tall woman with the red hair?"

"She's married to a policeman, and she's helped me before. Not only that, but she follows Annie around and has access to local gossip."

Minoru shrugged, and Jack could see how his time abroad set him apart. "We'll see. Can we meet here day after tomorrow?"

After he and Jack had parted ways, Minoru returned to the park where Minami-san's body had been discovered. A team of officers had scoured the area on hands and knees. They never missed anything, and Minoru was confident that any and all evidence had been found. He was excellent at his job and had a high success rate, so he didn't really think he needed Jack's help.

Sitting in the woods, he thought about Jack's careful observation and his quick diagnosis of possible causes of death. *Having a medical examiner on hand at the scene of the crime could certainly be helpful.* If he was completely honest with himself, however, his interest in Jack was more personal than professional. He had a vague idea that Jack could be helpful to his career in some way. Plus, he liked him. He wasn't too pushy or condescending but seemed to really want to help.

As he sat quietly contemplating the scene and his internal motivations, he noticed a disturbance in the soil behind one of the trees, perhaps six meters from the place where the victim had been found. He stood and approached the area, his pulse racing at the sight of a single footprint. He laid a cloth tape measure next to the print and took a photo with his mobile phone, then stepped back and took another showing the distance from the crime scene. Radioing junior detective Mori, he sat again to wait.

On his way back to the house, Jack stopped at a small grocery store to purchase a bottle of wine and at a flower shop to buy his grandmother a bouquet. *I came to meet my grandparents and haven't spent any time with them. I wish I could communicate with them.*

He entered the house a few minutes later, removing his shoes and calling, "Tadaima."

"Okaeri," five voices called from the living room.

Jack walked through and handed Oba the bottle of wine before approaching his grandmother and handing her the flowers. "Douzo," he said with a little bow.

Accepting them with a happy grin, Obaa-san began speaking a mile a minute.

Annie approached and said, "Grandma says thank you so much. They are very beautiful."

"It sounded like a lot more than that. Could you tell her that I came here to meet her and feel bad that I haven't spent any time getting to know her? I wish I could speak Japanese."

Annie relayed his message to his grandmother, and she took his hand with a gentle look on her face, speaking quietly, her eyes looking suspiciously moist.

"Obaa-san is so happy you are here. You remind her of your mother. She wishes she could have been part of your childhood, but she wasn't able to communicate with your father."

Jack nodded sadly. "He was not the same after mother died. I'll keep studying Japanese, so next time I visit, I'll be able to talk to you."

Ojii-san, sitting next to his wife, looked stern and unmoved, but Jack saw him place his hand on his wife's when a tear escaped her eye. He wanted to hug them, but he had never seen anyone in the Akiyama family hug, so he kept a reign on his emotions.

Glancing at Sam, sitting at the dining table sipping coffee, he was almost undone. The look on her face was too much, so he rose and excused himself, claiming that he needed to visit the facilities. Annie interpreted, and his grandparents nodded.

Remembering to change slippers, he locked the door behind him and sat on the toilet seat, blinking rapidly. He was sure that no grown Japanese man would ever be seen crying, and he didn't want to cause a lot of discomfort. He was adept at bottling up his feelings, and after a few minutes, he washed his hands and splashed some cold water on his face before rejoining the family.

"Gohan," his aunt called as he re-entered the living room.

Sam had collected herself and watched Jack out of the corner of her eye as she chatted quietly with Annie. She felt distraught whenever she thought about Jack's childhood and all that he had lost when his mother died.

She turned her attention to Annie, who was staring at her expectantly. "I'm sorry. I was lost in thought. Did you say something?"

Laughing, Annie repeated her question. "Takashi and I were wondering if you'd like to join us and two of our friends for a night out."

"It's up to Jack, but I'm game."

"Me too."

Oba waved them off after dinner, assuring Annie that she could take care of the cleanup, so they met up outside with Keiko Shima, Izumi's daughter, and Akio Minami, who, despite his father's recent death, seemed in good spirits. The six of them were all in their twenties, and all spoke English to varying degrees, so Sam and Jack were able to relax and decompress.

"Are they a couple?" Sam whispered to Annie.

"No." She giggled. "They tolerate each other because of Takashi and me."

"They look good together." Sam eyed Keiko's long, shiny hair and carefully made-up face, then glanced at Akio, who was tall and muscular. He had a handsome face and bleached hair, reminding her a little of some of the K-pop idols she had seen on TV.

"They do, but their personalities are a train wreck."

<hr>

The establishment they went to was more of a bar than a pub. Although the patrons were young and lively, and the karaoke system was given a workout, it wasn't as noisy as the bars back home, and there was a distinct lack of smell. The group sat at a table in a far corner before Takashi and Akio went to the bar and asked for bottles they had purchased on previous visits, whiskey, and rum.

When they returned to the table, they were followed by a server with a tray of glasses and a pitcher of water.

"Annie likes whiskey and water, but you can get other things to mix if you want," Keiko said. "I like Coke in mine."

"I'd like that too. Should I get us some?"

Keiko nodded at Sam. "Thank you."

"Does anyone else want anything?"

"I'll have a Coke, too," Jack said.

It occurred to her, as she made her way around the dozen or so tables, that she didn't know how to order. Jack had used kudasai, and she imagined Coca-Cola was universal. Holding up three fingers, she said, "Coca-Cola kudasai," and was rewarded with three bottles of coke. She tried to hand the bartender some 1,000 Yen notes, but he smiled and shook his head, pointing toward her table.

While Sam was at the bar, Akio went up to a small stage and began singing a catchy song she had never heard before. He was very confident, flamboyant, and obviously a crowd favorite. When she returned to the table, she set the bottles of Coke down and sat next to Jack. "I like that song. What is it?"

"It's called *Honky Tonky Crazy*." Annie giggled. "Akio-kun is a big Bowwy fan."

"Are there English songs too?"

"Oh, yeah. They have everything."

Akio strutted back to the table amidst loud applause and took a big swig of whiskey.

Annie stood next and approached the stage to more applause. She searched through the selections, chose her song, then grinned when the music began. She sang *Always* by Bon Jovi, and although she wasn't as charismatic as Akio, Sam thought she sang very well. Leaning toward Jack, she whispered, "Should we sing something?"

He wrinkled his nose. "I don't know."

"What if I can find something in Spanish?"

"It would probably be something really old if they have anything at all."

"Let me look."

Sam wandered up to the stage as Annie was finishing her song.

"Are you going to sing?"

"I don't know. Jack might sing with me if I can find a Spanish song."

Annie's brow furrowed. "I haven't ever heard anyone sing in Spanish here, but that doesn't mean they don't have it."

After searching for a while, Sam did a little dance on her toes. She selected the song she had found and motioned for Jack to join her.

"No way," he mouthed as he saw her selection. "*El Jefe*? You'd better own this because I can't do it justice."

"We'll try to do it like the video. It'll be a hoot."

Sam began by doing her best impression of Shakira, and Jack did his Fuerza Regida.

At first, the entire bar was silent, but then their friends got up and began to dance, and by the time they were finished, everyone was on their feet. They had started an impromptu dance party. To keep the ball rolling, Takashi ran up and selected *Uptown Funk* by Bruno Mars, and the party continued.

Hours later, when the bar closed for the night, the six friends wove their way home. They were sweaty and still laughing about the great time they had.

"We need to take you with us every time. That was the most fun I've had in ages," Annie declared. "Where did you learn how to sing in Spanish?"

"Our fathers were Mexican. It's in our genes."

"Shakira, Shakira." Akio laughed and wiggled his hips. "It's in your jeans."

"Don't be rude," Keiko said.

"I'm not rude. That dance was sekushi." He wiggled again.

Keiko rolled her eyes.

They said goodnight outside the Akiyama house and went their separate ways.

Once back in their room, Jack said, "We have a lot to discuss. Morning walk?"

Sam nodded and fell across her futon, which was not as soft and bouncy as her bed at home. "Ow," she mumbled before she fell asleep.

Chapter 9

Sam woke at six to find Jack dressed and sitting on his futon, staring into space. Rubbing the sleep from her eyes, she stretched and yawned. "How long have you been awake?"

"I don't know. I woke up thinking about the case and couldn't get back to sleep."

"Let's head out, and we can share info." She pulled on a pair of jeans and turned to change her shirt. "Ready." Turning back, she caught Jack staring. "What?"

He shook his head. "Nothing. Let's go."

They quietly put their shoes on and left through the front door, heading toward the beach.

Neither of them said anything for a few minutes, then Jack asked, "Have you talked to Tom since we came here?"

"I e-mailed him when I got here, but he didn't answer. He wasn't happy about me coming."

Jack nodded. "Our last conversation wasn't very positive, but he's usually pretty easy going." He paused. "Have you been happy with him?"

Sam was silent for a moment. "Mostly. It's weird. We both have conflicting wants, I think. He wants to support my survival school, but he wants kids right away. I want kids, too, I think, but I also want to do things." She gazed sadly at Jack. "You know how I am."

"I do."

"I thought Tom did, too, but I'm starting to wonder."

They had reached the shore, and Sam sat to remove her shoes. Looking up at Jack with anguish, she said, "He said no for the first time when I told him about this trip.

"He has expressed disapproval before, but he has never told me I couldn't do something."

Jack raised his eyebrow.

"He said if I came, he might not be there when I get back."

"And you came anyway?"

"First, I promised you a long time ago that I would. And second, I won't have someone trying to control me. If he leaves because of this, he isn't the man I thought he was."

"I'm so sorry, Sam."

"Hopefully, he was just overreacting, but if this is his true personality, I made a big mistake. It's hard to imagine that I could have been that wrong about him."

<hr>

Jack looked away. He didn't want Sam to see the hope in his eyes. "Let's talk about the case. We've been invited to meet with Inspector Ito tomorrow afternoon, and we should be on the same page."

"Okay. You start."

"When I met with him yesterday, I found out that his boss doesn't want me involved, which is not surprising."

"Does he know how Oba's scarf ended up around Minami-san's neck? Or why he was in the park so early in the morning?"

"So far, he hasn't told me anything, not even the official cause of death. What did you find out in Annie's English class?"

Sam told him about the local gossip, then said, "It will be interesting to hear what Ito has to say."

They sat in companionable silence, watching the waves roll in until a raised voice floated toward them on the breeze. "Jyaku! Samu!"

Turning to see Takashi jogging toward them, Jack was surprised that he hadn't even broken a sweat. His straight black hair flopped up and down above a headband, and his athletic attire showed off his broad chest and short, thin legs. *The Brazilian genes must have been strong. I look more like Sam than Takashi, and we aren't even related.*

"You should run with me in the morning."

"We enjoy our walks, but thank you for inviting us."

Grinning and jogging in place, Takashi gave them a little wave. "See you at breakfast."

"Jogging never appealed to me." Jack watched him run down the beach.

"Me neither. There are so many other things that are much more fun. I miss Ghost."

"You two belong together. I bet she misses you too."

Sam smiled at him. "This trip is worth it. Ready to head back?"

"Yep. I'm getting hungry."

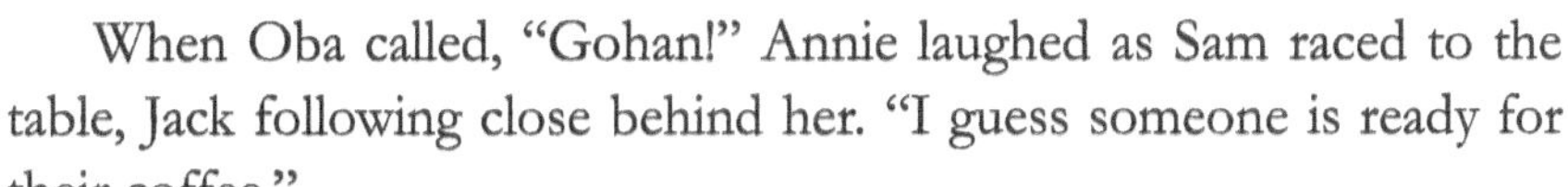

When Oba called, "Gohan!" Annie laughed as Sam raced to the table, Jack following close behind her. "I guess someone is ready for their coffee."

"Yes, pleeeease." Sam sat at the table and held her hands out.

"Something about prolonged partying stokes the morning hunger, doesn't it?" Annie handed each of them a cup of coffee and went back for their breakfast. Looking through from the kitchen, she said, "Are you ready for an outing? We've officially begun Golden Week."

"We had a good time in Hamamatsu. What do you have planned today?" Jack asked.

Joining them at the table, she said, "There are so many possibilities. What are you interested in? We could visit local shrines; the gardens are beautiful this time of year. Or maybe you like amusement parks? Shopping? We could wander around a small town. I'd like to take you to Kyoto, but the police told us not to travel. I can't figure out why they haven't come to interview us yet."

"I don't really know Japanese investigative protocols, but I'm sure they're following them. Will the whole family be coming with us today?"

"It depends on what we decide to do."

"What do you think, Sam?"

"Let's go see some shrines."

"Done. I'll see if the others want to come."

"I'd like to treat everyone to lunch if you know of a good place."

"You don't have to do that, Jack."

"Humor me, please."

"Well, let me get you more coffee, then I'll see if I can convince everyone that we need a group outing."

"Will that be difficult?" Sam accepted a second cup of coffee.

"Like herding cats."

"You always seem to get the brunt of it."

"No worries. I'm really enjoying your visit." Annie bustled off.

"It's almost like a void forms when she leaves."

"Like you." Jack sipped his coffee.

"No, like *you*." Sam nudged him with her shoulder.

"Hey. Watch it, or you'll make me spill my coffee."

Everyone, including Jack's grandparents, squeezed into the family's minivan. Takashi drove, and Annie acted as a tour guide. "That's the supermarket I was going to take you to the other day and… Oh! We have to take them to a convenience store, Takashi. They are so different here. And *Mos Burger!* There's the post office. I used to walk everywhere before we got married. I was very fit."

"You need to run with me."

Annie made a face. "Here we are."

Takashi parked near the base of a short, cement staircase.

Staring up at the bright orange gate towering above them, Sam ran straight into Jack, who had stopped to offer his arm to his grandmother. *She doesn't seem to need any help. She's pretty spry for her age, but Jack's attention is making her happy.* She smiled to herself.

Approaching the shrine, she watched Oba and Grandma light sticks of incense, then everyone took turns pulling a thick rope to ring a melon-sized bell, clapping twice, and bowing their heads.

"Go ahead and ring the bell," Annie said, "then say a little prayer."

Sam did her best to mimic the small ritual, then looked inside the shrine and wandered around inspecting the statues that dotted the grounds.

Annie appeared at her elbow. "Takashi and I got married here. I'll show you the photos later if you want. Come on, you'll love the flower park." Annie took Sam's hand and made her smile again as she practically skipped along the path in her excitement.

They turned a corner, and Sam gasped. Enormous bushes covered in a profusion of flowers, pinks, lavender, and white, all demanded her attention. "They're gorgeous!" Sam looked around for Jack but didn't see him, so she followed Annie through the rioting flowers.

The path wound like a maze, but Annie knew her way and exited into a serene oasis of green. The gentle, rolling lawn, surrounded by pines and weeping willows, encircled a wooden bridge spanning a small pond. A sigh escaped her lips. "If I was an artist, I would want to paint this. Oh, who am I kidding? I want to paint it anyway, but I could never do it justice."

"We took pictures on that bridge." Annie gazed at it with a little smile. "There's another place I want to show you, but we should probably have lunch first so Ba-ba and Ji-ji don't get too tired. Here they come now."

Inspectors Ito and Mori began their day early. Their first stop was at the Hirano home. Daiki answered the door in neat brown trousers and a button-down shirt. Politely inviting them inside, he led them to the living room where his wife, Asami, sat wanly on a cushion in front of a low table with a large, ornate shawl around her shoulders. Daiki offered them seats and then left the room, returning with tea.

Inspector Ito accepted a cup of tea out of politeness and glanced around the room.

The house was very old, but the green of the tatami mats showed they had been replaced, and the furniture was of good quality. "I imagine you've heard about Minami-san. We would like to ask you a few questions." Daiki gazed at him without expression, so he continued. "I understand that you worked for him until recently."

"Yes, that's true."

"Were you angry when he let you go?"

"It was not ideal, as my wife is unwell, but he gave me a good severance package and a reference."

"May I ask why?"

"We had a difference of opinion."

"About what?"

"A business matter."

Ito waited for him to continue, but that was all he would say on the subject. "Where were you at seven o'clock yesterday morning?"

"We were still in bed. We get up at eight."

Asami, who hadn't moved or acknowledged them in any way, gave a brief nod of her head.

"Just one more question. Do you know of anyone who hated Minami-san enough to harm him?"

"He was not well-liked."

"So, I gathered. But was there anyone who hated him?"

Mrs. Hirano, staring at the table, startled him when she spoke, her voice surprisingly strong. "You should begin closer to home."

After a moment of silence, Ito rose, followed by Mori. "Thank you very much for your time. We'll show ourselves out."

The Hiranos remained at the kotatsu as the inspectors returned to the entryway and retrieved their shoes.

Outside, Ito said, "What do you make of that, Keibu-ho?"

Mori shook his head. "Nothing there, I suspect."

"Let's go talk to the Shima family."

"Why are we skipping this house?" Mori asked as they walked by the Akiyama residence.

"Two reasons. First, they don't appear to be home. Second, I want you to interview them while I interview their guests. I've set up an appointment with them for tomorrow."

"Couldn't we just interview them all at the house?"

Feeling a slight twinge of concern at this uncharacteristic questioning of his decision, he glanced at Mori, who was studying his feet. "They are foreigners, and one is a medical examiner. I don't want them interfering."

Mori didn't reply but followed his superior to the next house.

⁂

When Izumi Shima answered the door, the energy she radiated was almost shocking in contrast to the Hiranos. She invited them inside, pulled out slippers for them, and called to her husband with a merry, ringing voice as she led them to the living room. Politely offering them seats on a modern sofa, she asked if they would like tea.

"No, thank you. I think we've reached our quota." Ito again scanned his surroundings and found that although the Shima house was also old, the décor was lively, suiting Mrs. Shima's personality perfectly.

"This is my husband, Goro," she said as he entered the room. "How can we help you?"

Introductions made, Ito said, "I'm sure you've heard about Minami-san."

"Oh, yes. His poor family."

"We're investigating his death and would like to ask you a few questions."

"Of course," Goro said. Unlike his wife, he was businesslike with a closed expression, but Ito could sense their amicable relationship.

"Is it just the two of you living here?"

"No, our daughter Keiko-chan lives with us. Do you want to speak with her too?"

"Yes, is she home?"

"I'll go get her. Just a moment please." Izumi bustled out of the room, and the three men sat in silence until she returned with Keiko, who was still in her pajamas, her long hair in disarray.

"I'm very sorry to disturb you, Miss Shima."

She sat on the floor, facing the sofa, and waved a hand in front of her face to indicate it was no bother, then accepted a cup of tea from her mother.

Once everyone was situated, Ito began again. "Please tell me where you were at seven o'clock Thursday morning."

"My wife was making breakfast, and I was preparing to open the shop," Goro said.

"Did you see anyone outside?"

Goro nodded. "Annie-chan and her guests parked outside the Akiyama home and went inside, then the guests left and walked toward town."

"Did you see them return?"

"No, I came in for breakfast after that."

"What time did you open your shop?"

"I always open at eight."

"Did you see anyone at that time?"

"No."

Ito looked at Keiko.

"I leave for work at seven-thirty, so I had toast and coffee while mother was making breakfast and left while she and father were eating."

"Did you see anyone outside?"

"I saw Sam, a guest next door, leave the house. She was running, and by the time I pulled out of the driveway, she was gone."

"Can you describe her?"

"She's very tall and has red hair."

"You didn't see anyone else?"

"No."

"Do any of you know who might have hated Minami-san enough to harm him?"

They looked at one another.

"No one liked him," Goro said.

"Why?"

They gazed at Ito with blank faces. "He was not a nice man."

"We are talking about murder. Would someone kill him for not being nice?"

Keiko was looking silently at Ito. "His wife hated him because he was having an affair."

"True," said her mother. "Or maybe his mistress killed him."

Goro, not to be outdone, said, "He fired Hirano-san, but he would never kill anyone. He's a good man."

"What about his son? Did they get along?"

"It's hard to know what Akio-kun is thinking… if he thinks at all."

Izumi looked at her daughter sharply.

"You don't like him?"

"Not particularly. Minami-san was trying to make father agree to a marriage."

"You said no?" Ito looked at Mr. Shima.

"I told him the young people could marry if they wanted to, but I wasn't going to force my daughter into an unhappy union."

"Did he threaten you?"

"He was always threatening everyone. I didn't listen to his nonsense."

"What did he threaten?"

Goro was silent for a moment. "He insinuated that something bad might happen to Keiko." His voice was so quiet that Ito thought he might have misheard him, but he knew he hadn't. The hairs on his arms stood on end.

Keiko stared at her father, and her mother put her hand on her chest. Goro didn't meet their eyes.

"Thank you for your honesty. Is there anything else you can think of that might help us?"

"Father wouldn't have killed him," Keiko said.

Ito observed her for a moment, then stood. "Thank you very much for your time. We will be in touch if we have any more questions." Mori put his notebook away and stood as well, trailing behind as Mr. Shima led them to the entryway, bowing as they bid him farewell.

"Any thoughts, Keibu-ho?"

"He had motive but no opportunity, I'd say."

"We'll keep him in mind, but I agree. Let's head back to the station."

Chapter 10

After some discussion, the Akiyama family decided to take their guests to a large ramen shop for lunch.

"It's part of a chain, but still quite good," Annie explained as they entered.

The staff helped them push several tables together and handed them menus once they were seated.

Jack had been teaching Sam her numbers, so when it was her turn to order, she said, "Doku kudasai." The waitress stared at her with a blank look, so she pointed to number six on the menu and repeated, "Doku."

The waitress gave a slight bow and left hurriedly. Annie grinned as they heard the staff laughing in the kitchen.

"What?" Sam asked.

Snickering, Annie said, "You asked for poison."

"Oh, no! How do you say six?"

"Roku."

Jack's shoulders were quaking with suppressed mirth, and Sam blushed. "So much for my attempt at speaking Japanese."

"No worries. Everyone makes mistakes when they're learning a language. I've made some whoppers, but that was a good one. Give me some poison, mate." Annie laughed.

The rest of the family remained politely quiet, and the waitress, when she returned, had regained her composure. Number six was a soy sauce-based soup without fish cakes, and Sam had ordered a side of gyouza as well.

"Did you write down how to make these?" Sam asked Jack.

"I did, but we'll have to find out where to buy the wrappers if we don't want to make them from scratch."

"Can we take some home with us?"

"I don't think they'd last the trip."

Disappointed, Sam took up her chopsticks and soup spoon and began to tackle her enormous bowl of ramen.

"Don't worry. I'm sure we can find some in Albuquerque."

"Ba-ba and ji-ji want to home after lunch." Takashi had been speaking quietly with his parents and grandparents at the far end of the table.

"Can we still go see the wisteria after we drop them off?"

"Yes."

"Are your parents coming?"

"Just mother."

Annie nodded.

Etsuko, it turned out, was the life of the party once she got away from her husband and his parents. She smiled a lot and tried her best to speak in English. Jack could see that she had a naturally social nature and that she liked Annie. They walked beneath a long trellis covered in lengthy strands of flowering purple and white wisteria. "Kirei desu ne. So pretty."

"So desu ne. This is one of my favorite places." Annie gazed up at the beautiful lavender flowers.

"Isn't it interesting how much beauty you can find looking up? Is that on purpose?" Sam said to no one in particular. "I'm going to get a crick in my neck."

"Remember when you took me on that hike to show me the land up close?" "It's kind of the opposite here, isn't it? All the details are on the roofs and gates and in the trees."

Annie interpreted for her mother-in-law, who nodded sagely.

"This nagafuji eight hundred old."

"Years," Annie added. "This wisteria tree is eight hundred years old."

"Amazing." Jack watched the many visitors milling around and sitting on benches beneath the wide trellis, noticing their deep appreciation of nature's beauty. *Like Sam. She takes the time to really look at things.*

"Maybe tomorrow we can visit the tulip park. You came at a lovely time of year. If you visit again, make sure you come in autumn. That's wonderful, too."

Jack's mind was boggled. "It would take years to explore just one little area in Japan."

"True. I'm certainly no expert on anything, but I do know Iwata quite well by now. We should probably head back home. Where did Takashi disappear to?" Annie scanned the crowd and then pulled out her phone. Her phone pinged in response, and she glanced at it. "He ran into some friends. He'll meet us in the car park."

Sam's stomach rumbled loudly. "What's for dinner?" she asked, causing Annie to laugh.

"That's why you should eat all your noodles."

"They make me really full, and then I'm hungry an hour later."

"I make chaohan," Etsuko said unexpectedly. "You have snack home."

"What's chaohan?"

"Fried rice. You'll love it. Etsuko's chaohan is the best!" Annie linked arms with her mother-in-law and chatted with her on their way to the car.

Sam and Jack sat at the dining table with Takashi, nibbling on crackers and drinking beer, while Annie helped Etsuko in the kitchen. "What would you be doing this week if we weren't here?" Sam asked.

Takashi thought about that. "Sometime we travel. Annie like to visit Australia. We have work cleanup, too."

"Can we help with that?" Jack asked.

Waving his hand in front of his face, Takashi said, "No. You holiday. Me. Father. We work sometime."

Sam picked up another cracker. "Are the schools closed this week too?"

"Yes."

"What do the kids do during Golden Week?"

"Many people travel. Very busy train and hotel."

"And flower parks, it seems." Jack smiled.

"Yes. Annie like flower. She say tomorrow chuulippu."

"Tulips," Annie said from the kitchen.

"Gohan!" Etsuko called as Annie entered to clear the table.

⁂

Sam still struggled with letting them wait on her. Oba went so far as to gather her laundry every morning and leave it clean and neatly folded on her futon. Sitting in her place at the table, she watched the others. Grandma, who had surely been the one to cook and clean in the past, was now free to enjoy being served by someone else. *I wonder if it was a difficult transition.* Then she thought about Annie. *One day, Annie will take Oba's place. Maybe after she has children?* She wondered how that worked but didn't want to ask. *Annie already has misgivings about her future.* She tried to picture living with Tom's family and being responsible for running her mother-in-law's home, and she shivered.

"Is everything okay?" Jack asked.

"Yes. I'm fine. Dinner smells wonderful."

When she had been told they were having fried rice for dinner, Sam had pictured a plate of soy sauce-flavored rice like you might expect at the Chinese buffet, but she should have known better. She surveyed the many bowls placed in front of her. The chaohan, in the shape of an upside-down bowl, was artistically placed on a small plate, and accompanied by miso soup. Four smaller bowls, almost plates with shallow sides and about the size of her palm, contained shredded salad, pickled vegetables, and thinly cut, marinated beef.

The family didn't wait, picking up their chopsticks, and intoning, "Itadakimasu," as the food appeared in front of them, but Sam and Jack waited until Annie and Oba had joined them at the table.

Sam was getting better at using her chopsticks but had asked for a spoon. She knew there was no way that mound of rice would end up in her mouth if she tried to eat it with chopsticks. Jack, she noticed, was making a good effort.

She took a bite of rice and chewed. "This is amazing," she told Annie. "Not what I expected at all." The many types of finely chopped vegetables and eggs added texture, and the flavor was complex. "What all's in this?"

"What isn't?" Annie chuckled. "The flavoring includes soy sauce, mirin, dashi, sesame oil, chicken consume, salt, and white pepper. Maybe other stuff; it's not always the same."

"What are mirin and dashi?"

"Mirin is a sweet rice wine, and dashi is… fish essence? We use it in the miso soup, too."

"Can I buy them at the store to take home with me?"

"I'll point them out next time we go."

"That reminds me, we were going to ask Takashi to show us where the myoga grows."

"Yes. I show you on the beach. That my secret ingredient for miso soup."

"How do I say it's delicious?"

"Oishii desu."

Sam said, "Chaohan oishii desu, Oba-san. Is that right?"

Annie smiled. "Close enough."

Oba grinned. "Thank you, Sam."

<hr>

"Gochisousamadeshita." Not a scrap of food was left on the table. Jack's grandparents moved to the sofa to watch television, and Takashi told Sam, "Please take a bath."

"Yes, sir." Sam chuckled as she got up from the table. Jack remained with Takashi and Oji. Annie had brought the beer and snacks on a return trip from the kitchen, and Oji poured.

Takashi's father was a quiet man, his complete lack of expression causing him to appear taciturn, but Jack suspected this was not the case. "Could you ask your father if he has any memories of my mother he'd like to share?"

Takashi interpreted Jack's question, and Oji observed Jack from across the table. *He doesn't look like my mom. His eyebrows are so heavy and dark, and his face is long and square. I wonder what she would look like now.* He didn't remember her well but kept her picture on his bedside table at home.

After taking a sip of beer, Oji set his glass on the table and began to speak, Takashi doing his best to interpret for him.

"I do not think of her for many years until you come. She was very beautiful and always fun. We—" He paused. "We have happy children."

"Had a happy childhood," Annie corrected from the kitchen.

"We play on the beach and ride bicycles. She have many friends." He took another sip of beer, and Takashi poured more into their glasses. "I was lonely when she went."

"That was when she was in high school?"

"Yes. She was older. I was in junior high school. When she return before university, she not the same. She didn't have time. It was last time I saw her." Oji's face didn't change, other than a slight tightness around his mouth, but Jack saw the regret in his eyes. He said something else, and Takashi glanced at Annie in the kitchen.

"We always think there will be more time," she supplied.

Oji took another sip of beer. "It's a pity. You lost her when you were very young."

"Yes. It changed my life."

Sam returned from her bath, and Jack, taking his turn, was grateful to be alone with his thoughts.

"What happened?" Sam accepted a glass from Annie as Oji excused himself and left the room.

"Jack was asking about his mother," Annie said.

Sam didn't know what to say.

Takashi poured beer for her, and Sam thought she understood the tiny glasses. *Small portions of everything. I wonder what they'd think of our Thanksgiving dinner. I should invite them.* She frowned. *I wonder if Tom will be there.*

Annie joined them at the table, and Oba went upstairs. "Is everything okay?"

"Yes. I was just thinking. There's so much to process, visiting for the first time." She poured for Annie and Takashi.

"When I first came to Japan, I was intrigued; every day was a learning experience. I felt kind of like you do, probably. But after about six months, I got really bad culture shock. It didn't happen right away, so I wasn't expecting it, and it was so bad I wanted to go home. I asked my boss if I could break my contract, and he said no."

"I'm happy you stay," Takashi said.

"Me too, mostly."

He looked at her questioningly, but she was looking at Sam.

"I've heard of culture shock, but I don't really know what it means."

"I suppose it means something different to each person who experiences it, but for me..." She stopped and swirled the beer around in her glass. "I suddenly realized that everything I thought to be true wasn't. I had been taking my acquaintanceships at face value, mistaking politeness and interest for something deeper. I realized that I didn't understand anyone around me and that they didn't understand me either. It's hard to explain, but I suddenly felt lonely and isolated and so deeply unhappy that I didn't want to be here anymore."

"How long did that last?"

Annie laughed. "I don't remember. Not too long. I remember how I felt when it hit, but at some point, it just went away."

"It sounds terrible. I can imagine, though, that after all the initial excitement of being in a new place and learning so much in a short period of time… once the excitement starts wearing off, you might miss the life you're used to?"

"That was part of it. But realizing that I didn't have any real connections with my students or my boss or anyone really, that was the hardest part."

Jack entered the room and said, "I'm headed for bed. I've finished my bath if anyone else wants to have a soak."

"I'll hit the hay as well." Sam stood. "Thank you both for a marvelous day."

"You're very welcome. We had a nice time, too. See you in the morning."

— ·•◦⟨⟨⟩⟩◦•· —

Annie was waiting for Takashi when he went upstairs to bed. "We need to talk."

"You have been very quiet." He sat next to her on the side of their Western-style bed.

Feeling her anger and resentment welling up inside her again, Annie closed her eyes and took a deep breath. "I've been unhappy. Your mother is talking about children, and you're never around, especially when I need you. I don't want to turn into a bored housewife by the time I'm thirty."

Takashi remained very still, searching her face with worried eyes. "Don't you love me anymore?"

"I do love you, but sometimes I think it's not enough. I feel trapped in someone else's life."

"I don't know what you want me to do." He paused. "I am worried about Minami-san's murder right now. Can we discuss our future after this is over?"

Annie didn't want to put it off, but she bit her tongue and nodded. "Why are you worried?"

"The police have been asking everyone where they were that morning."

"You were running, weren't you?"

"Yes, and I saw a stranger on the beach."

"That seems lucky. What did they look like?"

"She was a foreigner. She sat in the sand next to a blue bicycle with a white basket. The wind was whipping her long, blonde ponytail around her face. I turned back after I passed, wondering if I should ask if she needed help, but she was already pushing her bike in the opposite direction."

"Did you see her face?"

"Not clearly. She was too far away. I don't think they will believe me. At least you have an alibi."

Annie shrugged. "I guess so. I'm going to sleep now." She climbed under the covers and turned her back to him. *There's always a reason why we can't sort things out.*

Chapter 11

The next morning was uneventful, and Ito was waiting in the izakaya when Jack and Sam arrived. He stood and rather than bow or shake hands, did an awkward combination of both. When the three of them were seated, he poured beer into their glasses and asked if they had eaten lunch.

"No, the family doesn't usually eat until later. I told them we'd be eating out."

"You didn't tell them we were meeting, did you?"

"No." Jack noticed Ito's shoulders relax slightly.

"Keibu-ho Mori will interview the family this afternoon."

"What does keibu-ho mean?" Sam asked.

"Junior inspector. He works for me."

"Does he know you're meeting with us?"

"I told him I am interviewing you. Let's order, and then we can go through your movements that morning." He signaled the server, then watched Sam with awe as she ordered half the menu.

"Sorry. I want to try everything."

Jack took his turn pouring beer.

"Tell me about that morning. What were you doing in the park?"

"We got back from Hamamatsu early because Annie had to get ready for her classes. No one was around, so we decided to take a walk."

"I went to the park with Annie on Tuesday and wanted to show Jack the cool slide. Then, afterward, we were going to see the shrines she said were at the end of the path."

"We never made it to the shrines because we found Mr. Minami's body. I stayed with the body and asked Sam to run to the house and get someone to call the police."

83

"So, you ran all the way to the house?"

"It's not very far."

"What happened when you got there?"

"I hollered for Annie, and she came downstairs in her housecoat. Then, I told her what happened, and she said she would call and then get dressed. She asked if I wanted a ride back, but I said no, that Jack was there alone. So, I ran back to the park and got there shortly before you did."

"What did you do while you were waiting?"

"I scanned the scene of the crime and did a superficial examination of the body. I was careful not to touch anything after I felt for a pulse."

"So, neither of you saw anyone else during that time?"

"Takashi arrived home from his run at the same time we returned from the park, and his mother was making breakfast when we went inside."

"You didn't see anyone at the park? Or on your way there?"

Sam had been silent during the last two questions, but to this one, she said, "We saw a few shopkeepers preparing to open, but I don't think we saw anyone we knew."

"I just remembered. I saw Oji and Mr. Shima greeting each other and heading for their shops as we were leaving on our walk. I was going to wave hello, but they weren't looking in our direction."

"Did you see them, too?" Ito asked Sam.

"No, I was looking the other way."

"We had a couple of questions, too," Jack said.

Ito remained silent but nodded slightly.

"Have you determined the official cause of death?"

"I included your opinions in my official report, but the police doctor said strangulation. He said an autopsy would verify his findings, but it's not necessary. The victim is currently on ice, and I am advocating for an autopsy."

"Did you find out how that scarf ended up around the victim's neck?"

"No, but several neighbors identified it as the property of Etsuko Akiyama."

"She couldn't have been in the park that morning, so…"

"Why do you say that?"

"Because she was at home making breakfast."

"Are you sure? You said you didn't see her until you returned."

Jack stared at him. *Our relationship has somehow shifted. What's he up to?* He glanced at Sam. "We were also wondering what the victim was doing in the park at that hour. Did he have a habit of taking early-morning walks?"

"No. In fact, his family reported that he had been feeling unwell. They were surprised to hear that he was found in the park." Ito paused. "Have you learned anything?"

Sam poured the beer and glanced at Jack, who answered.

"The neighbors were upset about some of his activities."

"Can you be more specific?"

"This is hearsay, but apparently, he was trying to get some beachfront property rezoned. Everyone I've talked to seemed upset about that. And he recently fired a man whose wife is receiving expensive medical treatments."

"Yes, I heard about that. Anything else?"

"Annie's students said that his wife hated him," Sam added.

"He was also trying to trick your grandfather into selling his property."

Jack raised an eyebrow. "That must have been what they were arguing about."

"Tell me about this argument." Ito sat up straighter.

"I couldn't understand what they were saying."

"Who?"

"My uncle was speaking with Mr. Minami, and something about their body language was unfriendly. Then, my cousin joined them, and their voices got louder, so I went over to see if they needed some help, but Takashi told me it was a 'family matter,' so I left."

"When was that?"

"Last… Tuesday?" Jack looked at Sam, who nodded.

"I must go now. Thank you for your help. We'll talk again." He stood abruptly and, with a slight bow, left the izakaya.

"That was strange. He didn't even eat anything."

"More for you," Jack said. "Something has changed. Does he suspect someone in the family?"

"I hope not. I hope it wasn't a mistake telling him about that argument." She picked up a rice ball that had been grilled in soy sauce and took a bite. "I love these. Do they have doggie bags here?"

"I don't think so. I've never seen anyone taking their leftovers."

"We'd better eat it all then. It would be a shame to waste it. Why are these glasses so small? They only hold about a quarter cup of beer."

"Maybe it's so they can enjoy this pouring ritual in large groups." Jack refilled Sam's glass and his own.

Sam frowned. "Maybe it's harder to monitor your beer consumption."

Jack wasn't really paying attention; he was busy puzzling over Minoru's change in attitude. *What would make me suddenly stop sharing information with someone?* He could think of several reasons, none of them good.

"You're putting me off my food, cuz. Why don't we just go?"

"I thought you didn't want to waste it."

"There's no sense eating it if we can't enjoy it. We'll come back another time." She looked at him with concern. "I know you're worried. Let's go see what's happening."

The house was quiet when they returned. Removing their shoes, they called "Tadaima" and heard several mumbled responses from the living room. The entire family, minus Takashi, was seated like a grouping of stone statues. Annie's face was very pale, her eyes bloodshot and puffy from crying, but the other family members wore shuttered, stoic expressions.

They sat together but alone with their thoughts.

Sam sat on the edge of the dining platform next to Annie and whispered, "What happened?"

Rising, Annie motioned her and Jack to follow. She led them into their guest room and closed the paper doors, then sat with them on their futons. She clasped her hands and looked at Sam, then at Jack, and took a shuddering breath. "They've taken Takashi in for voluntary questioning."

"At least they didn't arrest him," Sam said.

"This might be worse."

"I've heard horror stories about 'voluntary questioning.' Are they true?" Jack asked.

"I think so. I'm so worried. And I feel so guilty for how I've been acting toward him."

"Let's try to stay focused. You can mend your relationship when he gets home. Tell me what happened before they took him."

"Four policemen came, and one stayed in the living room with us while two interviewed each of us separately. I think one of them was searching the house."

"What did they ask you?"

"They showed me a picture of Etsuko's scarf and asked me if I had seen it before. Then they asked questions about whose it was, where I had seen it, if she had mentioned it being lost…"

"What else?"

"They asked if I knew of anyone who hated Mr. Minami."

"Did you answer truthfully?"

Annie nodded, then looked at her hands, twisting her wedding ring round and round. "They asked me if Takashi hated him. I said hate was a strong word, but that he was unhappy about how he was treating Ji-ji."

Jack nodded, but Annie wasn't looking at him. She was staring off into space. "They asked about his morning runs." Her voice shook. "He told me he had seen a girl on the beach that morning, but he didn't know who she was. Maybe they can find her—if they look."

"Did the policemen ask you anything else?"

"They wanted to know where I'd been, who I saw, what they were doing. It's hard to remember exactly, but I told them about returning from Hamamatsu and getting ready for my classes and how you came back to the house and asked me to call the police." Annie looked at Sam. "Did they question you, too?"

"They asked us about our movements when we found the body but not about the family."

"From what I've heard, if they've taken him in for voluntary questioning, it means that they think he committed the crime. And if that's so, they'll be seeking a confession and won't be looking at other suspects. We'll need to put our heads together and try to find some compelling evidence. Tell me about the girl on the beach."

Jack's questions helped her focus on facts rather than emotion. She thought back. "It was a weird conversation because we had been having an argument, and we weren't speaking much. Somehow, we ended up talking about proving where we'd been because of the murder, you know, and he said there was a mystery girl on the beach. I thought he was just making it up at first, but he described her. She was a foreigner."

"Are there many foreigners around here?" Jack asked.

"Not too many. She was by herself and had a bicycle, so she probably lives around here. Not in this little part of town, but she might work at the school I used to work at. I could ask around."

"Finding her would help."

"The murder seems premeditated, doesn't it?" Sam interjected. "I mean, the killer took the scarf to the park. And did they arrange a meeting, or was the killer following Mr. Minami?" Her brow furrowed.

"He had been unwell, according to his family, and wasn't in the habit of taking morning walks. I think we can assume he was meeting someone. I think he was probably in a weakened state, so the killer could have been a woman."

Eyes wide, Annie gaped at Jack. "How do you know all that?"

"Ito shared that bit of information before I became persona non grata. I wondered why his attitude changed. Now, I know."

"You said Mr. Minami might have been poisoned, right? Who would be in a position to do that?"

"Someone he saw daily who had access to his food or drink. I don't know anything about his household, but his wife would be the most likely person."

"She hated him, but if she did poison him, what does that have to do with the strangling?" Annie asked. "Was it taking too long?"

"We need more information. We can't even be sure what he died from. It could have been either. Let's start with the girl on the beach. If we find her, that will give me an excuse to meet with Ito."

"I'll drive over to the school now. It will give me something to do other than worry." She stood. "You know how you kept wanting to help around the house? Tonight might be a good night for you to share one of your recipes with the family."

"We're on it." Jack grinned.

"Just visit the Shima's shop next door if you don't have everything you need."

Ito joined Mori and Takashi in the interview room. He didn't personally approve of the methods they used to coerce confessions, but they were effective in most cases and were necessary evils in his profession. Keibu-ho Mori had waited for him, and when he entered the room, Takashi looked toward him with wide eyes.

Beginning gently, Ito said, "We have proof that you were in the park at the time of Minami-san's murder and witnesses to your altercation on Tuesday. Did you kill him because he was trying to cheat your grandfather?"

"I wasn't in the park, and I didn't kill him. I was running on the beach like I do every morning. I told Keibu-ho that I saw someone there."

"A very convenient story. Did that person also see you?"

"Yes."

"Who is this person?"

"I don't know. I've never seen her before, but she's a foreigner."

"You were very angry with Minami-san for trying to trick your grandfather into selling his land. Did you try to poison him?"

Takashi gawped at him. "How would I poison him?"

"Why did you strangle him when you were already poisoning him?"

Opening and closing his mouth like a fish, Takashi was shocked into silence.

"Why did you use your mother's scarf?"

"My mother's…"

"Taking the scarf with you to the park indicates that the crime was pre-meditated. How long had you been planning his death?"

"I… I would never… I wasn't even in the park. I told you."

"We have a cast of your footprint at the scene."

"You can't because I wasn't there."

"You were, and we can prove it. It will be much better for you if you confess now. The judge will be more lenient, and your sentence reduced."

"I swear I had nothing to do with his death, and I was nowhere near the park."

Ito stood. "I've heard enough. Carry on," he told Mori before he left the room.

⁕

Walking back to his office, he frowned. Truthfully, he had his doubts. Although the footprint was the same size as Takashi's, they had not found a shoe with the same tread in his possession.

Ito needed time to think about the information he had and cringed internally when Keishi Fukuda called to him as he passed his office. "Keibu, I need an update. Has the perpetrator confessed?"

"No, Keishi."

"Put more pressure on him."

Taking a steading breath, Ito stuck a toe into dangerous waters. "I'm not convinced of his guilt, Keishi."

"The evidence is clear. That foreign doctor has muddied your thoughts. You will face disciplinary action if you have any further communication with him. Do you understand?"

Ito stood stiffly, taking shallow breaths. He could feel sweat popping out along his hairline. "Yes, Keishi."

"Now, get back to work."

Once safely locked in the men's room, Ito splashed water on his face and stared at his pale reflection in the mirror above the sink. *A rock and a hard place is what the Americans call it. What do I do now?*

Annie realized the English school was closed for Golden Week, so she drove to the apartment building where most of the Australian teachers lived. Knocking on her friend Rhonda's door, she heard cheerful voices and raucous music coming from inside. The door was opened by a pale young man with a riot of carrot-colored curls and the greenest eyes she had ever seen. He grinned like the Cheshire cat and drawled, "G'day, mate. What can I do ya for?"

"Is Rhonda about?"

"Nah. She's on holiday. I'm Jim."

"I wanted her help finding someone."

"Come on in and have a cold one." He held the door open. "Cut the music," he hollered, and the sudden silence was deafening. "This sheila needs our help, mates."

"Sorry for interrupting. My name's Annie, I used to work with Rhonda." She accepted the can of beer Jim handed her. "I'm looking for a girl who was on the beach with a blue bicycle last Thursday morning. She had a long blonde ponytail, and her bike had a white basket with plastic flowers."

"Is she in trouble?"

"No. She might be able to provide an alibi."

"Crikey!" He looked at his friends. "We've a couple of sheilas with long blonde hair, but I don't know what kind of bikes they ride. We could check around."

"Ta. My husband saw her on the beach when he was jogging, and she's the only person who could say he was there."

Looking slightly disappointed, Jim held out his hand for her phone and texted himself. "I'll pass her your number if we find her."

Annie thanked him again and left, hoping he and his friends would be able to help. She sat in her car, trying to slow her racing heart. *Where is he? What are they doing to him? Will they let him come home? Does he know I love him?* She took a deep breath. *Focus. I need to focus.*

Chapter 12

Jack's aunt, uncle, and grandparents went to lie down while Annie was away, so he and Sam put their heads together and decided to make grilled chicken, mashed potatoes, and asparagus for dinner. "It's simple, but hopefully they'll like it."

"I'll make a salad," Sam said, pulling vegetables from the refrigerator. "I wish we could make them Mexican food, but we'd need to find some spices. Did Annie tell Oba we're making dinner?"

"I hope so."

Annie returned, calling "Tadaima," and entering the living room at the same time as Oba.

"Okaeri," Oba said absently, then froze when she saw Sam and Jack in the kitchen. She stared in horror before speaking adamantly in Japanese.

Annie responded in a placating tone and led her to the sofa. She walked quickly to the kitchen. "I told her I'd make her some tea. I should have let her know you were cooking." Pumping hot water out of the electric pot, she quickly filled a teacup and dropped in a bag of green tea. "I'm for it now."

"Did you find the girl?" Sam asked.

"Not yet. I'll tell you about it after dinner." Annie carried the cup of tea to her mother-in-law and sat next to her on the sofa.

"This must be the worst-timed visit in the history of visits," Jack mumbled.

"It might be the luckiest. At least you're here to help."

"I wish I could do more. If we find that witness, I'll at least have a toe in the door." He looked up as Oji entered the living room with his grandparents. "Gohan," he called.

Oba looked up with a frown, but Grandma smiled and clapped her hands as she made her way to the dining table.

"Please apologize for the simple meal, Annie, and let Oba know that we were just trying to make this difficult time a little easier for her."

Annie interpreted, and Oba nodded resignedly. "Doumo, Jyaku-kun. Very kind."

Jack carefully plated the dinner and Sam filled individual salad bowls, then they carried them to the table, starting with the grandparents' meals, then aunt and uncle, and finally Annie's and their own.

Obaa-san, eyes twinkling, said something to Annie, who interpreted. "Grandma says it looks delicious." She picked up her fork and said, "Itadakimasu."

"Itadakimasu," everyone repeated before taking their first bite.

Sam knew from experience that everything Jack cooked was delicious, so she wasn't surprised that dinner was a big hit. What *did* surprise her was how Oba relaxed and seemed to be enjoying herself as the meal progressed.

⁓

After dinner, Oba shooed Sam and Jack away and reclaimed her spot in the kitchen. No one seemed very social, so they decided to take a walk.

Finding themselves at the bar they visited the previous night, they decided to stop for a drink. Akio was up on stage again when they sat at the bar, and although he had seen them enter, he didn't approach them to say hello after his performance.

"He must have heard about Takashi," Sam said.

"It's a small neighborhood."

The bartender approached them, and it occurred to Jack that he didn't know how to order. "What do you want, Sam?"

"Rum and coke?"

The bartender seemed to understand what she said, so Jack held up two fingers.

"Do you speak English?" Jack asked when the bartender returned with two drinks.

"Iie, iie." He waved his hand in front of his face and smiled.

Jack smiled back and picked up his drink. "Doumo."

Sam picked hers up as well and took a sip. "Not bad. How's yours?"

"Pretty good. I don't usually drink anything other than beer, but I thought tonight might be an exception."

"And last night."

"I forgot about that." Jack chuckled.

<hr>

Sam lay awake that night, thinking about Annie and Takashi and her husband Tom. *If anything happened to him while I'm away, I would never forgive myself. I need to try to make things right and let him know I love him.* She got up and went outside with her phone. He didn't answer, but mobile service in Santo Milagro was spotty at best, so she sent him another e-mail, then she went back inside and crawled into her futon.

She closed her eyes and prayed. *Lord, Please look after Tom and be with Takashi and Annie through this ordeal. Help us uncover the murderer so they can be together again. In the name of the Father, the Son, and the Holy Spirit, Amen.* She crossed herself and fell into a fitful sleep, her eyes popping open again several hours later.

She had no idea why she woke but got up and wandered into the living room, where she saw Annie sitting with Oba and Grandma at the dining table, surrounded by hundreds of paper cranes. "What are you doing?" She sat next to Annie at the table and picked up one of the colorful cranes.

"We are making senbazuru, a thousand cranes, to make a wish for Takashi's safe return."

Sam gaped. "That's a lot of cranes."

"It's believed that long ago, cranes lived for a thousand years and that they can grant wishes. Would you like to help?" Annie handed her a square piece of origami paper."

"Can you show me how?"

"Sure. Mine aren't as beautiful as theirs. Their lines are so crisp and precise. Start with the white side up and fold it in half diagonally, matching up the corners." Demonstrating, she ran her fingernail along the fold to make a sharper edge, and Sam copied her.

"Then fold it in half again."

She continued, step by step until they each held a completed crane. Sam felt pleased with her first attempt, but when she compared it to Oba's, she understood what Annie meant.

Pointing at the crane Oba had just completed, Sam asked, "How does she get it so perfect?"

"I have no idea. Japanese women have some kind of superpower. It's the same when they wrap gifts or make gyouza." She shook her head.

"I'll do my best." Sam picked up another piece of paper. "How are you keeping count?"

"We're making piles of twenty, then combining them into piles of one hundred."

Sam nodded and started folding. By the time Jack wandered into the living room, they had four hundred, including those made before Sam joined them.

"What are you doing?" Jack echoed Sam's question and ended up sitting at the table to help as Annie went to make coffee.

The spell was broken when Oji entered the room. "Nani yatteruno?"

Oba got up quickly and hurried into the kitchen as Annie leaned toward Sam and Jack. "He just asked what we're doing. Why don't you go ahead and get dressed. I'll help Oba get breakfast ready. Thank you for helping with the cranes."

Monday was a long day. No one in the family had much enthusiasm, so Annie asked Jack and Sam if they'd like to go to the supermarket and out to lunch.

They drove to the store, and when they entered, Sam gaped. *It looks like a supermarket, but it's so different.* "It's so clean and organized." She watched shoppers with miniature carts line up at small, spread-out check stands. "Why...?"

Without waiting for Sam to articulate her thought, Annie said, "We buy what we need every day or two rather than buying groceries for a week. That way, we know our food is very fresh, and we don't need giant carts and long counters. Go ahead and look around while I shop. I'll meet you at the checkout counter in about half an hour."

Jack followed Sam through the produce department. "They sell things in smaller quantities, too." He picked up a small package. "What are these?"

Canting her head, Sam examined the two colorful, packaged items. They were about three inches long and cylindrical, slightly pointed at the ends. "I have no idea. We should ask Annie. There's a lot of stuff here I've never seen before."

They continued up and down the aisles, noticing the differences and similarities in inventory. At the far end of the store, there were racks of beautiful water glasses and teacups.

"I want to take one of these sets home for Melissa." Sam picked up a sturdy ceramic plate and matching cup. "They look handmade." The rectangular plate was long enough to place a small sweet next to the cup.

"She'll love them. How many are in the set?"

"Six, I think. Let's find Annie."

Annie, when they found her, was chatting with Yoko from her English class. "Thank you, Yoko-san. We'll see you this afternoon," she said before Yoko walked away.

Turning to Sam and Jack, she said, "Yoko knows the Minami family's housekeeper. She's going to bring her to talk to us later."

"That's great. Maybe we'll find out something important."

"Are you done looking around already?"

"What's this?" Jack held out the unusual vegetable he found in the produce section.

"Isn't that funny? Most people wouldn't even notice that. It's called myoga, Japanese ginger. Takashi likes to add it to miso soup, and guess what? It grows wild on the beach near our house. Maybe he can show you where to find it." Annie's face crumpled for a moment, then she sniffed and straightened her spine. "Right. Gambarimasu."

"What's that mean?"

"It's one of those words that can mean many things, but in this case, it means I will persevere. I'll carry on until Takashi is back home. I'm not helping anyone if I let my emotions take over. That's what Etsuko says, anyway."

Throwing her arm around Annie's shoulders and walking her toward the cups, Sam said, "Maybe Yoko's friend will help us figure it out, and we still have that girl from the beach, whoever she is."

"Where are we going?"

"I want to buy something for my friend, and I need your help." Sam grinned. When they got to the racks of cups, Sam pointed out the set she wanted.

Annie picked up one of the cups and admired it. "These are lovely; they give the impression of being sturdy and dainty at the same time."

"True." Sam studied the design, cream-colored with small, dainty flowers painted in pink. "Are they for coffee or tea?"

"I think you could use them for either. They're shaped like small coffee cups, but the tray… we often eat sweet, miniature cakes with bitter matcha green tea and the tray is the perfect size. You should take her some tea and cakes as well. You can try it at home so you can explain it to her."

Sam placed the tea set in Annie's cart and when they arrived at the check stand, the checker wrapped each individual item in paper and placed them in bags. *I also need to find gifts for Tom and Roger. I wonder what they would like.*

"Are you two hungry yet? I want to take you to my favorite fast-food restaurant."

"Sam's always hungry." Jack laughed.

"So are you." She elbowed him.

"Then get ready for something amazing. Next stop, Mos Burger."

At first glance, Mos Burger looked like any other fast-food restaurant. Wooden tables were accompanied by red, padded chairs, booths, and stools, and smiling staff behind the counter looked neat in aprons and caps.

Annie had assured them that the item they needed to order was the spicy Mos cheeseburger. The other selections, which were plentiful and diverse, were to be ignored. Jack thought maybe they could each buy two and try them all, but Annie insisted they try the spicy burger first. She ordered for all of them and was given a number. Leading them to a nearby table, she said, "They make everything to order, so it can take a while if they're busy."

When one of the staff delivered their burgers, Jack watched Annie before unwrapping his.

"How do we eat these?" Jack asked.

"Keep it in the envelope because it's really messy."

Sam gave hers a sniff. "What's on it?"

"They have some kind of meat sauce and a layer of jalapeños. It's the best." Annie took a big bite of her burger.

Sam and Jack glanced at each other and bit into their burgers, Sam groaning as her eyes rolled back. "Oh, man, this is amazing."

Jack nodded as he chewed thoughtfully. "The flavors are so perfect together.

"I love the thick slice of tomato; it adds a burst of freshness to the savory sauce. Is it chili?"

"They don't call it chili, but that's what it tastes like to me."

"Gosh, I wish we could take some home with us. Can we come back again tomorrow?"

"We'll see. Maybe not tomorrow, but before you leave." Annie took another bite.

"I want another one. How do I order it?" Jack stood.

"Say Mows shpy-she chee-zoo bah-gah." Annie laughed at his expression. "It'll work. Trust me."

"Get me one, too," Sam said.

"How do I ask for two?"

"Futatsu."

Jack approached the counter with trepidation, but the young man taking his order understood his request, quickly counted out his change, and gave him a number.

Returning to the table, he said, "I'm sorry, Annie. Did you want one, too?"

"No, thanks. I'm stuffed."

"One would probably have been enough, but they're so darned good." Sam opened her second burger when it arrived.

"This can take the place of fries."

"Mmmm."

"I love your enthusiasm, Sam. I'm so glad you like them."

Sam, busy chewing, vigorously nodded her head.

Chapter 13

After lunch, they found Oba and Grandma at the dining table, once again folding paper cranes. Sam and Jack sat to join them as Annie went into the kitchen to prepare tea for Yoko's visit. After she poured hot water over the leaves in the tea pot, she returned to the table and informed her elders about their imminent visitors.

Yoko knocked on the front door before opening it and calling, "Ojamashimasu. Murakami Yoko desu."

Annie rushed to the front door to greet her and was introduced to Sazaki-san, the Minami's housekeeper. "Please come in. Does Sazaki-san speak English?"

"No, I'm sorry."

"That's okay. I'll interpret for Sam and Jack." Annie switched to Japanese and introduced the two women to everyone around the table before bringing the tea.

"Senbazuru," Oba said, and both guests reached for origami paper and began to fold.

After Annie had served tea, she sat with them and addressed Sazaki-san in Japanese. She explained how Takashi was taken for questioning, and Jack was trying to find out the truth so he could come home.

After suitable commiseration, Sazaki-san began to speak about the family.

Interpreting for her, Annie told Sam and Jack that until recently, the house had been very quiet. "Yoshinori and his son, Akio, left early for work and often returned late. Kazue busied herself with her hobbies and volunteer work. Because they were rarely home, housework was light most days."

"What changed?" Jack asked.

Sazaki-san focused on her crane as she pondered his question. "The father began complaining of pain and staying home from work more often. He was very demanding, and his wife ran back and forth, taking him water and medicine and cooking. He accused her more than once of poisoning him, and as she got more tired and frustrated, she became unpleasant toward me."

"Have you ever seen Minami-san carrying around a little wooden box?"

"Yes, I often saw him holding it."

"When did you first see it?"

"When he began staying at home. Last month?"

"Do you know what was in it?"

"No. He hid it from me when I went in."

Jack picked up his phone and opened the gallery before passing it to Mrs. Sazaki. "Have you seen this scarf?"

"Oh, yes. The missus found it in the living room and said it belonged to Akiyama-san. She asked her son to return it for her since he often met Takashi-kun."

"Did you notice anything unusual in the house before Minami-san's death other than his illness?"

"Yes, one thing." Sazaki-san paused and looked at Yoko. "I don't know if I should say."

"Please do," Annie encouraged her. "Any information might be useful."

"A few days before he died, the father and son argued loudly. I was in the next room cleaning, and I overheard." She finished another crane. "Father said mother was poisoning him. 'If I die,' he said, 'you must run the company and continue fighting for the rezoning. Also, you must take care of Harumi-san.' That is when the shouting started. Akio-kun told him no. 'You are dishonoring our family, and I won't be responsible for continuing that. All of our neighbors hate us.'

"That made father angry, and he started yelling about how Akio-kun was lazy and ungrateful. They both said things they probably regretted."

Jack took a deep breath, letting it out slowly. "Please thank Sazaki-san. It looks like we'll need to interview Akio next."

It took her a little while to wind down after her big revelation, so Annie poured more tea, and they continued folding cranes while Yoko and Etsuko commiserated with her about her unfortunate position.

When Etsuko rose to begin preparing the evening meal, Yoko looked at her watch and exclaimed at the time. She and Sazaki-san said their goodbyes and thanked Annie for the tea.

"Thank you for your help. I'll see you in class next week," she told Yoko.

Returning to the kitchen, Etsuko waved her away and told her to help with the senbazuru.

"Where is Grandfather?" Jack asked.

"He's out helping Takashi's dad. They do deep cleaning and inventory during Golden Week. It's a good time to do things they don't usually have time for. Ordinarily, Takashi would help but, well," her voice hitched, "he's not here."

"He'll be home soon. Jack's a genius."

"Don't say things like that." He frowned. "That's a lot of pressure."

"Hey, if the foo shits."

"Whaaat?" Annie managed a crooked smile.

"Excuse me a minute. I want to make a phone call."

— · · ⟨✲⟩ · · —

Sam went into the guest room and sat down on her futon. Pulling up her contacts, she called Mick on his office phone.

"Dennis Mickelson," he answered.

"Hi Mick, it's Sam."

"Heyy, it's our world traveler. How's your trip so far?"

"It's fine. I'm calling because I'm worried about Tom. Is he doing okay?"

"He took a leave of absence when you left, and I haven't seen him."

Sam bit her lip.

"Sam? Are you okay? He didn't tell you he was going to take time off?"

"No. Let me know if you hear from him."

"I will. You let me know, too."

"Thanks, Mick."

Sam disconnected and sat there wondering where Tom went and what he was thinking, looking up when Jack entered the room.

"Everything okay?"

"I don't know," she said slowly. "I called Mick, and he hasn't seen Tom since I left."

Jack saw there were two ways he could answer, but he took the high road. "I'm sure he's just taking this opportunity to visit his family or do some fishing. Maybe he went to Vegas to visit friends."

"He didn't mind us hanging out at first. What happened between you two?"

"I plead the fifth. Let's just say I was upset, and he was pushing too hard."

"I hope we can work it out. I need both of you."

"I know. I'll try to mend fences when I see him again."

"Tadaima!" Oji and Grandpa called from the front door.

"Okaerinasai," everyone responded.

"All the little rituals are comforting in a way," Jack said. "You never have to worry about being ignored when you get home, or no one saying thank you when you cook them a meal."

"Yeah, but it's not really heart felt, is it? Since you have to say it?"

Jack shrugged.

"Is it almost dinner time?"

"Not quite. How are we going to interview Akio?"

"We'll get Annie to help. She's friendly with everyone, and she can tell him Takashi needs his help. Let's ask her after dinner."

"Should we be in there folding paper cranes?"

"No, they put them away temporarily. With everyone helping, I think we're at about eight hundred."

"My fingers feel a little stiff." Sam flexed her hands.

Oba finally called everyone for dinner. Annie helped her serve grilled fish in a miso marinade that Sam recognized from the supermarket, along with white rice, coleslaw, and corn soup. "Itadakimasu."

"Dinner is delicious, Oba."

"Thank you, Sam." Etsuko smiled.

The meal was eaten mostly in silence, but Annie's phone rang toward the end of the meal, and she excused herself, returning five minutes later with a big grin. "We found her."

She spent several minutes explaining to the family, and the sudden transformation in their demeanor was startling.

Hand on her chest, Oba said, "Yokatta."

Both grandparents smiled as they released the tension that had been holding their spines erect. Oji jumped up and went into the kitchen, brandishing a bottle upon his return. He talked non-stop while he waited for Oba to bring a tray of shot-sized ceramic cups, then she took the bottle into the kitchen and traded it for a ceramic pitcher the size of a tall water glass. Oji poured a small amount of liquid into each cup.

"O-sake," he told Jack. "Kampai!"

"Kampai," everyone repeated.

Sam, involuntarily shuddering as the sharp taste of sake hit her throat, hoped they weren't celebrating precipitously. *Will an alibi automatically release Takashi from suspicion?* Glancing at Jack, she realized that he was wondering the same thing.

After dinner, Oba took over the kitchen, shooing the young people away, so they retired to the guest room to hear Annie's story. She told them about her visit with the Australian teachers and about her phone call. "A girl named Hannah called and said she was at the beach Thursday morning and saw Takashi. She agreed to talk to the police if it would help."

"Good. I'll call Ito and set up an appointment to see him. Is there anything else that might strengthen our case?"

"He couldn't have known about the poison," Sam said.

"And Takashi wouldn't have used his own mother's scarf," Annie added.

"Was there anyone Mr. Minami trusted? Someone he would agree to meet with in the park?"

"I didn't really know him. We still have to interview Akio-kun. He would want to help Takashi; they're best friends."

Sam shifted her weight on the futon. "How was his relationship with his father other than that argument? He didn't seem very upset when we went to karaoke."

"You would have to ask Takashi. Japanese family relationships are rarely what they seem." Annie paused, and her eyes seemed to lose focus for a moment. "I had a businessman in one of my advanced classes who never showed any expression in class and always said terrible things about his wife. He said she was ugly and a terrible cook. I was sure he hated our class, but one day, he invited me to his house for dinner. His wife was a lovely woman, so shy and charming, and she made an absolutely delicious meal. I sat at the table and was blown away by the obvious affection they shared. I mean, I could see that he adored her, and I wondered why he would talk so badly about her in class."

Sam canted her head to one side. "Did you ask him?"

"No, but I asked Takashi. He said that it would be considered bad form if he bragged about her, but other men of his age and position would understand that he was saying the exact opposite of what he thought."

"Do Japanese women do the same thing? What about Mrs. Minami?"

"I think…" Annie paused. "Well, two things. One is that there are certain things you can say and some that you can't. Saying that your wife can't cook or your husband is a slob is par for the course, but saying something really personal isn't done. The other thing is that my students seem to think that English class is a safe space. They tell me things they would never tell anyone else."

"Like what?"

"Once, Kazue told me she hated her husband so much that she couldn't stand touching his underwear, so she removed it from the washing machine with a stick. She didn't tell me about his affair, but Minami-san wasn't careful, and everyone in the neighborhood knew."

"I wonder if the police have questioned his mistress?" Jack said. "Is she one of your neighbors?"

"I think she's his secretary, but I'm not sure."

"Then Akio would know her."

"Probably."

Jack made a little list and showed it to Sam and Annie. "At least I'll have some things to bring up when we meet. I'll call him and make an appointment."

<hr />

He walked outside and called the number on Minoru's business card. Although it was after business hours, Ito answered on the second ring. "Hai. Keibu Ito desu."

"Hello, Ito," Jack said. "I have some information for you. Could we meet?"

After a short pause, Minoru said, "I have been forbidden to speak with you because of your connection to the Akiyama family."

"I could come to the station, and you can have another officer present if you like. I have found a witness to corroborate Takashi-kun's alibi, and I have some additional information about the victim's family."

"I'm sorry. I can't."

Jack disconnected and returned to the guest room feeling dejected. "He doesn't want to meet."

"Did you tell him we found the witness?" Annie asked.

"Yes, I did."

"They have to listen. What do we do now?"

"Let's continue gathering information, then I'll request a meeting with Ito's boss."

"And if that doesn't work?"

"I think it will, but if it doesn't, we'll find a lawyer. And who knows; maybe Ito will change his mind once he thinks about it."

Ending his call with Jack, Minoru felt a heaviness in his chest. *If he has proof of Akiyama-san's alibi, we need to hear it.* He tried to think of a way around his superior's directive but was at a loss. *Would it count if I sent Mori to interview him? No, Keishi would find out. The only thing I can do is find the real killer.* He remained at his desk, puzzling through the information he had.

Arguably, Akiyama Takashi-san was not an idiot. He would not take his mother's scarf to commit murder. Also, he had a point about the poison; if there was poison involved. The autopsy was scheduled for the next day, and Minoru hoped that it would provide the information he needed.

Ordinarily, the public was extremely helpful when interviewed about a crime, but no one would care to implicate themselves. He and Mori had spoken with the widow who, according to everyone in the neighborhood, despised her husband. Although she did not feign immense grief, she also did not speak of him in a disrespectful manner. His son, while carefully shielding his mother, spoke frankly of the neighbors' anger toward his rezoning campaign.

Other than his family, Minoru wondered who could have been poisoning the victim. Several witnesses had mentioned a mistress. *Is it possible that the widow and son didn't know about her? I wish I had asked them.*

Resting his chin on his hands, Minoru began to doubt his own ability for the first time. He knew in his heart he was a good investigator, but he also knew they had the wrong man.

Sam, Jack, and Annie returned to the dining room and sat down with Oba and Grandma to fold more cranes. "This is sure time consuming," Sam said.

"We're almost done, and then we can make our wish. Would you like some tea or a snack?"

"Hmm. What are our options?"

"Beer and crackers?"

"Sounds good to me. How about you, cuz?"

"Sure."

Annie went into the kitchen, returning with several kinds of snacks.

Picking one up, Sam examined it. "I love all the different kinds of food here. What are these?" The round, light brown cracker had a cream-colored circle in the middle. She took a bite. "Tastes like cheese. I love cheese."

Jack picked up a thick, round cracker with peanuts in it. "Is this a cracker or a cookie?"

"That's sembei, which is translated as rice cracker. Most of them are crunchy, but the peanut sembei is a little like a cookie, isn't it? I quite like them."

"Mmm. Try this, Sam." He handed her half. "We're not getting much folding done."

"That's okay. We can take turns helping while we take our baths. You go ahead, Sam."

"Thanks, Annie," Sam said. "I won't be long. I love that bathtub."

"Me too. If I ever have my own house, I want a Japanese shower room with one of those tubs."

Sam left to bathe while the others continued with their folding. When she returned, Oba and Grandma had gone to bed, so she sat down with Annie and told Jack it was his turn.

Annie, still busy folding, handed Sam a large photo album. "These are the wedding photos I told you about. I thought you might like to see them."

Sam opened the book and looked at each picture carefully. The first pictures showed Annie being dressed in a kimono and then posing with Takashi. "Do men wear kimonos too?"

"That is called montsuki."

"I like the white pom-poms in front." Sam turned the page to find pictures of the ceremony, inside the shrine, then pictures of the family, and finally shots of the newly married couple on the bridge Annie had pointed out. "The two of you look so happy. It was a beautiful ceremony."

"Yes." Annie ran her finger over a picture of herself and Takashi on the bridge. "I'm so worried about him." Her lip quivered.

"He's innocent. He will be okay."

Chapter 14

Tossing and turning that night, Sam had a strange dream. She was surrounded by black and white, red-crowned cranes with faces that resembled the people they had interviewed. One with a blank face held Minami-san's wing and said, "Cranes mate for life." A crane with Akio's face said, "He's not a true crane; he chose my mother first." All the other cranes surrounded Minami-san, chanting reasons why he wasn't a real crane, and then all of them became silent as a crane with Tom's face entered the circle and stared at Sam. "I'm a true crane. Have faith in me, Sam." That's when her eyes popped open. *Tom. I love you, Tom. Please be okay.*

She tried to get back to sleep but couldn't. Laying there with her eyes open, she thought of her husband and all he had given up for her. Coming to Japan with Jack was the only thing he had ever objected to. *Maybe I was being selfish, but I needed to repair our relationship. Was I wrong? If Jack had given me more notice, we might have been able to talk through it. I wonder what happened between the two of them.*

At six, she got dressed and wandered into the dining room. Grandma smiled at her and held up the senbazuru, all strung neatly and tied together. "It's beautiful. Kirei."

Annie and Oba were in the kitchen getting breakfast ready. "Tell Jack to get up, and we'll make our wish together."

Jack was awake when Sam went to get him. "I'll be there as soon as I get dressed. Save some coffee for me."

"Aye, aye, captain." She saluted and went back to the dining room.

Annie brought her a cup of coffee when she sat. "Toast or fish?"

"Toast, please."

Jack entered the dining room, and Annie set his coffee in front of him.

Grandma gained everyone's attention when she began speaking.

"It's time to make our wish," Annie interpreted. "We should all be clear on what we are wishing for. How about Takashi's safe return home soon?"

"That sounds perfect."

"I agree," Jack said.

Annie interpreted for Oba and Grandma, then they all held hands and made their wish.

Grandma smiled and looked at Jack. "Gambatte kudasai."

"Do your best and accomplish your goal," Annie told him.

Jack nodded. "Hai."

"Gambarimasu," Annie said.

After breakfast, Annie drove Jack and Sam to the Minami electronics factory for their interview with Akio. He went outside to meet them, then ushered them through the security checkpoint and down a long hall that echoed their progress. They entered an office to the left, and Akio found chairs for everyone before calling for coffee through the desk-top intercom.

Jack scanned the room. "Was this your father's office?"

"Why do you think so?"

"It just doesn't seem your style." Jack grinned.

Akio glanced around at the heavy, dark furniture and the overt opulence his father favored. "It's not. I'm sorry to hear about Takashi-kun," he told Annie. "I've already spoken to the police, but how can I help?"

"We found someone who can verify his alibi, but Keibu Ito refused a meeting, so we're trying to find out as much as we can before requesting a meeting with his superior."

A middle-aged woman entered the office with a tea tray, placed it on the corner of the desk, and backed toward the door.

Jack observed her behavior, noting her black dress and the dark circles under her eyes. When she closed the door behind her, he refocused on Akio. "Was that your father's secretary?"

"Yes. How did you know?"

"She appears to be in mourning."

Akio pressed his lips together. "I suppose you know about them?"

Jack nodded. "What's her name?"

"Watanabe Harumi."

"How long has she worked here?"

"Ages. Ten years?"

"Will you keep her on?"

"I don't have a good reason to fire her other than I can't stand to look at her."

"So, the company will continue as usual?"

"Yes. Father mostly left me to run it anyway; he was always in 'business meetings' with Watanabe-san."

Jack thought he sounded bitter and couldn't really blame him. He glanced at Sam, surreptitiously taking notes, before he pulled out his phone and opened the gallery. "Have you seen this scarf before?"

Akio looked at the picture and nodded. "Yes, my mother found it at home and asked me to give it to Takashi-kun. I think it belongs to his mother."

"Did you return it?"

"No. I was on my way to work, and I forgot about it."

"When did you last see it?"

Akio breathed out through his nose and frowned, staring off into the distance for a moment. "I think I left it on this desk. I came in here to complain about something, and I got distracted. Father never paid attention to my suggestions. He didn't seem to care much anymore."

"Did you come back to look for the scarf?"

"No. I completely forgot about it. What's so important about the scarf?"

"Nothing, I guess." Jack returned his phone to his pocket. "You told the police your father had been unwell. What kind of symptoms did he have?"

"Symptoms?" Akio looked at Annie.

"Like cough, fever, signs of his illness."

"Ah. It was like influenza at first. Then he complained about pain in his stomach and in his feet. He told me he was dying, but I didn't believe him."

"Thank you very much for your help. Do you think we could speak to the foreman and the secretary before we go?"

"Yes. I will bring Ujiie-san first."

"Do you trust him?"

"Yes."

He spoke to Annie in Japanese for a moment, then left the office.

⁂

Annie watched him leave, then turned to Jack. "He said he didn't understand why you asked the questions you did, but he hoped his answers were helpful. He also told me that the foreman doesn't speak much English, so I'll need to interpret for you. And he asked if we'd like to have lunch with him after the next interview."

The door reopened, and a portly, bald man in overalls entered the office and bowed. "Ujiie desu." He sat gingerly behind the desk as if he shouldn't be there.

Interpreting for Jack, Annie explained their visit, and Ujiie-san, who must have been instructed to answer their questions, appeared cooperative.

"How long have you worked here?"

"Twenty years."

"Did you worry about your job when Minami-san died?"

Annie grimaced a little before she interpreted. It seemed like a very personal question, but Mr. Ujiie didn't appear bothered. "No, Akio-san can't run the factory without me. He doesn't know about daily operations."

Jack paused, "Did you have a lot of interaction with Minami-san?"

"We met every morning."

"In this office?"

Ujiie-san nodded and looked around.

"Did you like him?"

The foreman stared at Jack.

"Did you respect him?"

Again, silence. "He was my employer."

Changing tact, Jack pulled up the photo of the scarf again and asked the foreman if he recognized the scarf, surprised when he answered in the affirmative. "The scarf probably belonged to Watanabe-san. They were very close."

"Did you happen to notice him carrying around a little wooden box?

"Yes. I can't remember when I saw it. Not too long ago. It was sitting on this desk, and he kept fiddling with it. I wondered what was inside, but it wasn't my place to ask."

Jack nodded. "Do you use any dangerous materials in the factory?"

"Why is he asking that?" Ujiie-san asked Annie. "Wasn't Minami-san strangled?"

"Yes, he was," Annie answered.

He shrugged. "We do use some, like germanium, thallium, tellurium… only in small quantities, and we have a special room and protective gear when we work with them."

"If you needed to transport them or store them, how would you do that?"

"I wouldn't."

Jack gazed at him quietly, then pointed to a small glass container on one of the shelves. "What is that?"

Ujiie-san looked where Jack was pointing and swallowed. "It might be thallium."

"Why would Minami-san have it in his office?"

"I don't know, but it's sealed, so it should be safe. I should take it back to the laboratory."

"No, leave it here for now. Thank you very much for your help."

The foreman stood and bowed before heading quickly toward the door.

"That was interesting," Sam said.

Jack took a photo of the silver shavings.

When Akio returned, Jack asked him what was in the glass jar.

"That's a special metal used in production. The jar must remain sealed because it is toxic."

"Why is it in here?"

Akio frowned. "I don't know. I guess Father liked it for some reason. Sometimes he was… not very logical."

"Was that recent?"

"No, but he was getting worse. Would you three have lunch with me before you interview Watanabe-san?"

<hr>

A sudden hush descended on the large, on-site lunchroom when they entered. No one looked directly at them, but Sam could feel their scrutiny.

Akio said something in Japanese, and his employees resumed their lunches, although at a distance. He led his guests through the lunch line and told them to get whatever they liked, then paid the woman at the register before joining them at a table.

"Do your employees always react like that when you enter a room?" Sam asked.

"No, they haven't quite adjusted to my new status. I hope I'll regain their trust in time. What do you think of the food?"

"It's great," Jack said. "What is it?"

Akio laughed. "Yours is a bento. You should know that after staying with Takashi-kun."

"I was making a joke, although there are a few mystery items in here."

"I like this bun. I wish I had gotten two."

"That's nikuman. Try it with this sauce."

Sam took the bottle of brown sauce with a bulldog on the front and squirted some of it on the large, airy bun before taking another bite. The sweet, tangy, salty taste of the sauce, combined with the ground meat mixture, made her tastebuds sing. "I definitely need another one of these."

"Have you discovered anything useful today?" Akio asked Jack.

"It's hard to say what's useful and what's not. We're just collecting random information and hoping that something helps us figure out what happened."

"Your questions didn't seem exactly random."

"Not exactly, but somewhat."

"Who's that man in the corner by the window?" Sam asked. "He's been staring at us since we came in."

Akio scanned the room as he was eating. "That's Watanabe Harumi-san's husband."

"She's *married?*" Sam asked.

"Did you think there was only one cheater in that relationship?"

"Did he know?"

"It would be a miracle if he didn't."

"That's certainly a motive. Maybe we should interview him, too."

Eying the burly man's surly demeanor, Jack said, "Maybe it's better if the police tackle that one. What does he do here?"

"He works in the laboratory."

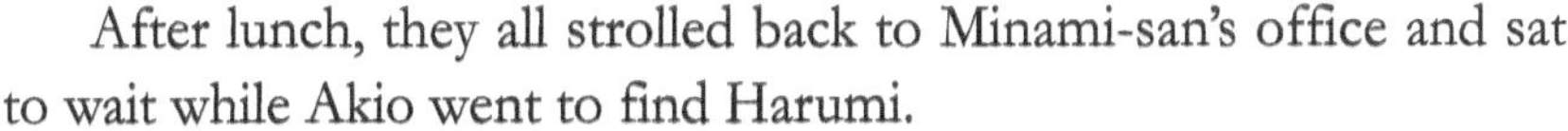

After lunch, they all strolled back to Minami-san's office and sat to wait while Akio went to find Harumi.

Jack glanced at the shelf, wondering if he should bag the jar of thallium shavings as evidence, but it was gone. *Interesting.* He looked toward the door when it opened and was surprised that Akio was alone.

"It seems Watanabe-san has left for the afternoon. I hope I won't have trouble with her now that Dad is gone. Could you come back tomorrow morning?"

"Yes, that's fine," Jack said.

"I'll text Annie if Watanabe-san calls in sick."

"Thank you for your time and for lunch."

"Anything I can do to help, just let me know."

He led them back through the building and said goodbye.

"I like him a lot better than the first time I met him," Sam said.

"He's a ripper, just has tickets on himself." Annie grinned.

"Do you think he likes Keiko after all? He might be putting on a show for her."

"If he is, he's going about it the wrong way. Keiko thinks he's a right galah. When are you going to try to make an appointment with the superintendent?"

"I was hoping we might know something by now. Let's go through our notes when we get home and see if we can figure it out."

Chapter 15

Beer was flowing in the Akiyama dining room. Daiki Hirano and Oji drank as they discussed Takashi's incarceration and the state of the Minami factory. Both looked up and intoned, "Okaeri," when Annie returned with Sam and Jack.

Surprised to see them in the dining room, Annie spoke to them before turning to Jack. "Hirano-san has something he wants to tell you." She went into the kitchen to get another bottle of beer and three minuscule glasses, then she took a seat and poured for everyone as Mr. Hirano spoke.

"He wants to help Takashi," Annie interpreted. "Minami-san fired him and gave him money to stay quiet. He needed the money for his wife's treatments, but since Minami-san died, he feels like he should speak up."

Jack raised an eyebrow and took a sip of his beer. "Has he spoken to the police?"

Interpreting again, Annie said, "He spoke with them but didn't tell them why he was fired. He worked as an accountant, and while he was going over the books, he found some discrepancies in the employee pension fund. That account showed a lot of debits, and he thought Minami-san should know right away."

Hirano-san's narrative stopped as he poured for everyone, and then he resumed.

"When he told his boss what he had found, Minami-san appeared angry and asked him to come to see him at the end of the day. Hirano-san thought his boss was going to look into the matter and advise him, but when he returned, he was asked to sign a non-disclosure form and given a severance packet."

Placing his glass on the table and leaning forward, Jack said, "The logical conclusion is that either Mr. Minami… or someone close to him… was withdrawing funds."

Annie interpreted, and Mr. Hirano nodded.

"He doesn't know if what he's telling you has anything to do with the murder, but Minami-san was a dishonorable man. Whoever killed him had their reasons, but it was nothing to do with Takashi-kun."

"Thank you, Hirano-san." Jack took his turn pouring. "Does Minami-san's son know about the missing money?"

"Probably not. Hirano-san has called to request a meeting; Akio-kun probably thinks he will ask for his job back."

"Will he?"

"He will accept if Akio-kun offers it, but he won't ask."

Jack nodded. "Please let me know how the meeting goes, and thank you for your help."

"It may not be connected, but he thought you should know."

"Every piece of information we get is helpful, so thank you."

As if someone had pressed his 'off' button, the shutters went down, and Mr. Hirano was finished sharing his personal business. He lifted his glass and turned toward Oji.

Dismissed, Jack stood and offered a hand to Sam. "Come on, we should go over everything we have so far."

"Let's go to my studio. It's more private than your room." Annie led the way out of the house and unlocked the door to her studio.

"Why do you lock the studio but not the house?" Jack looked around the serene room.

"The studio is kind of secluded, and when I first opened the school, things were going missing. People around here are usually honest, but some of my materials are expensive and hard to come by, so I decided to err on the side of caution." After pulling out a couple of chairs and placing a pod in her Keurig machine, Annie grinned. "This is my secret luxury."

Sam rubbed her hands together with glee, then opened her notebook.

Jack watched Annie's economical movements and her interaction with Sam. *They get along so well. I wonder if they're as different as they look.* "What kind of upbringing did you have, Annie?"

She placed Sam's coffee in front of her and started one for Jack. "What do you mean?"

"Town? Country? Big city? Private school?"

Annie laughed. "I grew up on a farm outside a small town. No private schools for me. My parents were always busy, so I was put to work if I looked idle." Smiling at the memory, she handed Jack his coffee and made one more cup.

"Do you ride?" Sam was suddenly very interested.

"Of course. I meant to ask you about your ranch. You mentioned it in class."

"It was the 'what do you do' question," she told Jack.

"She's also running a survival school. You should visit when you can."

"How did you manage the time to get away?"

"I have a super ranch foreman, and I scheduled the next survival camp a month out."

"I would love to visit sometime." Finally sitting with her coffee, she took a sip and nodded toward Sam's notebook. "What do you have so far?"

"I have notes from our interviews with the housekeeper, Akio, the foreman, and Mr. Hirano. They all seem to agree about the scarf, the wooden box, and Mr. Minami's general character."

"The scarf. Apparently, Oba left it at the Minami house. Does she go there often?"

Eyes wide, Annie tipped her head to the side. "She never goes over there. Kazue treats everyone like a huge inconvenience."

"Doesn't she have any friends? She must be lonely," Sam mumbled.

"I feel sorry for her sometimes, but she's a difficult person to like."

"So, how did Oba's scarf end up at her house?" Jack persisted.

"The only possibility I can come up with is my birthday party. A couple of months ago, all the students got together and threw me a party. Kazue hosted, and even the kids from my children's classes came with their parents. There must have been considerable planning involved."

"We can ask her. Put that in the notebook, Sam." Jack paused for her to write. "Kazue, or Mrs. Sazaki, found the scarf and remembered who it belonged to, so rather than take it across the street, she asked Akio to return it."

"Right. And Akio, when he spoke with his father in his office, set it on the desk and forgot about it. Why didn't Mr. Minami return it?"

"From what Sazaki-san said, that was probably around the time when he started feeling sick and stopped going to the office as much," Annie said.

"So, let's throw out some ideas about how that scarf got from the office to around Mr. Minami's neck." Jack stared into space. "He didn't take it back home because the foreman saw it on his desk."

"Maybe he thought it was his secretary's. He might have taken it home later so he could give it to her, or he might have left it for her."

Sam shifted in her chair. "What if she saw it and thought he was cheating? Did she know he was sick?"

"He must have let her know?"

"He didn't sound like a very considerate guy."

"We still don't know who took the scarf or where the wooden box came from. It must have been important since he carried it around with him and was holding it when he died. What else?"

"We don't know who was poisoning him or how. You're sure he was being poisoned?"

"It looks that way. I've seen those symptoms before."

"What about the pension fund? Do you think he was stealing money, or was he covering for his son? Or maybe his secretary? We should try to find out who had access to that account."

Sam looked at him and nodded. "I think we need to get more detailed information about his movements the week before he died."

"How do we do that?" Annie asked.

"Maybe his wife and the secretary can tell us."

"You don't want to interview them *together*?"

"No, but we can ask both of them and try to piece it together ourselves."

"It's probably dinner time. Let's head in so we don't get in trouble."

"What should we do with our cups?"

"I'll just soak them for now and wash them out later." Annie carried them over to the sink and filled them with water. "Ready? Maybe we can visit Kazue after dinner."

"Tadaima!" Jack and Sam echoed Annie when they entered the house.

"Okaerinasai. Gohan!"

The rest of the family members were already seated around the table, so they hurriedly joined them. "Itadakimasu."

Sam found her mind wandering as unintelligible conversation floated around her. She thought about Tom and wondered where he was, wondering if he still loved her. Startled by a sharp poke in her ribs, she said, "Oww. What was that for?"

Sitting next to her, Jack chuckled. "I called your name twice, and you didn't answer."

"I was thinking."

"Did it hurt?" Jack laughed at her expression.

"What's so important?"

"Oba was asking if you like your dinner."

"Yes. It's delicious." She had no idea what she was eating, but it tasted good and filled the void. "Didn't you say we were having Japanese pancakes?"

"Not today, it turns out. Are we still going over to see Kazue after dinner?" Annie asked.

"I'm really tired. Can we go tomorrow?"

"It's already Tuesday, and we're supposed to leave in a week. We should talk to her and try to make an appointment with Keishi Fukuda."

Sam sighed. "You're right."

Dinner wound up, and Annie explained their plan to the rest of the family, so Oba told her not to worry about the dishes.

"Gochisousamadeshita."

Annie stood. "Let's go."

⚫⚬⚫

They walked across the street and knocked.

Sazaki-san opened the door and offered them slippers before leading them across a wooden hall and into a tatami room with double paper doors on three sides. She invited them to sit at a low table, similar to the Akiyama's dining table, while she went to find Mrs. Minami.

Sam looked around. What she had seen of the house looked very different from the Akiyama home, which seemed to be a mixture of Japanese and Western influences. The Minami home was built in a more traditional Japanese style, even though it looked quite new. Curious as usual, Sam had a lot of questions that were unrelated to the murder.

When she entered the room, Kazue was well-dressed and perfectly made up, as if she had just returned from an important meeting.

"Ojamashimasu," Annie said.

Uncharacteristically, Kazue said, "Don't worry. It's no bother."

"As you probably know, Takashi-kun is being questioned by the police."

"Yes. What can I do?"

"Could you answer some questions for us? We are trying to gather information to prove Takashi didn't do it."

"What do you want to know?"

"Could you help us figure out your husband's movements during his last week? When he went to work, when he was home, if he went out anywhere?"

"That is difficult. Perhaps Sazaki-san can help us," she said as Mrs. Sazaki entered with a tea tray. "Sit here with me, please, and help me remember Yoshinori-san's schedule."

"I work Monday through Friday," Sazaki-san said in Japanese. She sat so stiffly Sam worried she might break. "Minami-san was out on Thursday, Friday, and Monday but in bed on Tuesday and Wednesday."

"Yes, I remember. Thank you. I don't know where he went on the days he was out, possibly work. He hobbled around the house on Saturday and Sunday, complaining of pain in his feet and demanding that I bring him food, blankets, medicine. On Monday, I was glad he wasn't home, but on Tuesday and Wednesday, he was here."

"We saw him speaking to Akiyama-san on Tuesday," Sam said.

"Sometimes he got up to do some little thing when his pain medication kicked in, but mostly he laid around."

Jack pulled up a picture of the scarf. "What day did you ask Akio to return Etsuko-san's scarf?"

Kazue paused. "Maybe it was Monday."

Did you ever see your husband carrying a small wooden box?"

"Yes. I asked him what it was, but he ignored me."

"Akio-kun said he accused you of poisoning him." Jack was fabricating, slightly, but it was for a good cause.

"Yes. That's funny since he kept yelling that I needed to cook for him. Before he got sick, he never ate at home."

"That's all our questions unless you can think of anything else?"

"No. He was a difficult man, but life will be strange without him."

Jack nodded. "Thank you for your help."

"I hope it does help. Takashi-kun is a nice young man and a good friend to Akio."

<hr>

"Her house is really interesting," Sam said as they crossed the street.

"When they rebuilt, Minami-san decided to keep the original style, with some minor upgrades, like western-style toilets."

"Japanese-style toilets are like the ones in the train station?" They had entered the house and changed their shoes before retiring to the guest room.

"Yes. Even though the one in this house was raised a foot off the ground, I am definitely glad they put in regular toilets. Anyway, maybe Kazue will give you a tour before you go. All of the rooms have paper doors, and the hall meanders around like a maze. I like it a lot."

"What's up, cuz?" Jack had been silent since they left the Minami house.

"Just thinking. What time are we expected at the factory tomorrow?"

"Nine o'clock. It's still early. Would you two like to go to the pub for a while?"

"By pub, do you mean an izakaya or that karaoke bar?"

"Wherever you want."

Sam grinned. "Let's go to the izakaya so we can eat something yummy."

"Let me check in with the family first, then we can go."

She left the room, and Sam glanced at Jack. "Is everything okay?"

"Yes. I'll call the station and make an appointment after we speak with Watanabe-san."

"Have you figured it out?"

"No, not exactly, but I have some ideas."

Annie returned, and they set off for the local izakaya.

Chapter 16

Annie was ready with coffee when Sam entered the dining room, then surprised her and Jack with scrambled eggs and pancakes.

"A feast! Where's Oba?"

"She has an appointment with her hairdresser this morning, so I told her I would make breakfast."

"It looks delicious." Jack picked up his fork. "Itadakimasu."

Sam waited for Annie to sit down. "Itadakimasu." She took a bite and nodded. "These are great. Do you have any syrup?"

"Oops. I forgot. Want more coffee while I'm in here?"

"Yes, please." Sam grabbed Jack's cup before she rose and carried both into the kitchen. "You don't have to wait on us while Oba's gone. We won't tell."

Laughing, Annie said, "It's been hard on you, hasn't it?"

"When I get home, I'll wonder where my servants are."

"Tom's got this," Jack mumbled.

Sam pressed her lips together as the remnants of her good cheer drained away. *I hope he'll be there.* They got resituated at the table, but Sam's appetite was gone. She pushed her food around on her plate and forced herself to eat a little.

"Come on, girl. I made a lot because I know how you like to eat. Don't you like it?"

"I'm sorry, Sam. I didn't mean anything by it."

"What? What's happening?"

"Nothing. It's fine. I'm just a little worried about Tom." She valiantly took a large bite of scrambled eggs and poured some syrup on her pancakes, then ran to the toilet room and threw them up.

After rinsing out her mouth and splashing some water on her face, she sat on the toilet with her head in her hands. *Oh, Tom. Where are you?*

Slowly walking back into the dining room, she saw that the plates had been cleared. "I'm so sorry, Annie."

"No worries. I've got a fresh cup of coffee for you."

"You're the best."

Jack hung his head and didn't meet her gaze.

"It's okay, cuz. It's not your fault. Well, it is, but I'm not blaming you." She elbowed him in the ribs.

"I was being a jerk."

"A little, but you didn't know it would make me lose my breakfast."

"Are you pregnant by any chance?" Annie asked with wide eyes.

"I didn't even think of that."

"No. I'm not."

"How can you be sure?"

Sam stared at Jack. "You're a doctor, right?"

"Point taken. I'll shut up now."

"Can I have my breakfast back?"

"I've scraped it all into the bin. How about I make you more when we get home?"

"Darn. Is it time to go?"

"Yes. Are you ready?"

⎯⎯⎯ ⋅⋅◦⥇∽⥆◦⋅⋅ ⎯⎯⎯

Once again, meeting them outside the factory, Akio shook Jack's hand and led the three of them through the security checkpoint and down the hall to Watanabe-san's office. He knocked as he entered and spoke to her for a few moments in rapid Japanese, then turned to Jack. "Please stop by my father's office when you've finished your interview. I have something I'd like to talk to you about."

Annie interpreted his instructions to Mrs. Watanabe and waited for Jack to begin.

"Thank you for assisting us with our inquiries, Watanabe-san. Our interpreter's husband is suspected in Minami-san's death, and we are trying to find out what really happened."

The secretary nodded silently. She still wore black, but the hollows under her eyes seemed to have decreased slightly.

"First, could you help us with this timeline of Minami-san's movements the week before he died?" Jack handed her a piece of paper that Annie had translated into Japanese.

Looking at the paper, Mrs. Watanabe showed a glimmer of interest. "Who gave you this information?"

"His wife and their housekeeper."

"It appears correct."

"When did you last see him?"

"On Monday."

"Is that when you gave him the small wooden box?"

Her mask slipped, and her face showed surprise for the first time. "No, I gave that to him several weeks earlier."

"What's in it?"

"I…"

"We know about your relationship with Minami-san, so please be frank."

"I don't know what was in it; it wouldn't open. My husband gave it to me, and I didn't want it. I thought it might remind Yoshinori-san of me, but after I gave it to him, I saw him less and less."

"And this scarf? Is this yours?" Jack showed her a picture of the scarf.

"No," she said coldly.

"Have you seen it before?"

"It was on his desk that Tuesday."

"Did you return it to him?"

"I didn't see him after Monday."

"Do you have access to any of the company accounts?"

"I can make deposits, but not withdrawals."

Jack nodded his understanding.

"Is there anything else you'd like to tell us? Anything unusual that you can remember?"

"My husband asked me to return the box."

"When was that?"

"I don't remember exactly, but I had already given it to Yoshinori-san."

Jack stood, Annie and Sam following suit. "Thank you very much for your help."

"Please," she said as they approached the door. "Could I have the box?"

"I will ask the police if you like."

"Thank you."

Minami-san's office was next door, so Jack led the way and knocked. Akio opened the door and ushered them inside. "Was Watanabe-san cooperative?"

"Yes, thank you. You have something to tell me?"

"Please, sit down." He sat behind the desk. "Hirano-san came to see me. He said he had already spoken to you."

"Yesterday."

"He told me why he was fired and that he wanted me to be aware of the problem. So, I went to see his replacement and asked him about it. He told me he was only given access to new files, nothing before Hirano-san's dismissal. I then asked him how he could do annual tax reporting if he didn't have files for the entire year, and he told me he isn't an accountant and doesn't do tax reporting."

"What will you do?"

"I will rehire Hirano-san and try to find the missing files. I could get into so much trouble over this. I wonder how much he stole."

"Mr. Hirano doesn't know?"

"He didn't get around to making a report because Father fired him. He said he noticed numerous small debits on a regular basis, and it worried him enough to tell Father immediately.

"I've asked him to keep it quiet and help me figure it out so I can pay the money back."

"Do you think he trusts you?"

"I hope so. I'm worried about what else Father might have done."

"Do you think he would have confided in Watanabe-san?"

"I have no idea how close they were."

"This is up to you, of course, but you might consider talking to a lawyer and notifying the tax authorities or whoever is in charge of pension funds. Let them know what happened and what you're doing to fix it."

"Why?"

"Because if someone else knows, they might try to sabotage your efforts or even blackmail you."

Akio closed his eyes and put his head in his hands. "Even in death, he is causing trouble.

"Is there anyone, other than your father, who had access to the funds in that account?"

"I'm not sure who the official signers are, other than myself and possibly Watanabe-san, but theoretically, anyone could complete a transaction if they held the inkan."

Jack glanced at Annie.

"It's an official signature stamp. No one can open an account without one."

After returning home, Jack excused himself and telephoned the police station, asking for the superintendent.

"Fukuda."

"Olivares Jack desu. I would like to meet with you."

"Chotto matte kudasi." The line was quiet for so long that Jack thought he might have disconnected, but eventually, a voice came through. "Ito desu."

"Hello, Ito, this is Jack. Since you refuse to meet with me, I thought I would set up an appointment with your boss. I can bring an interpreter if he likes."

"You're a bastard, Jack."

"If only you knew. Tell Keishi Fukuda that I have a witness to Takashi's alibi and have collected considerable information from local witnesses. If you don't set up this meeting, I will come to the station unannounced with the witness, a lawyer, and local media. It is time you release him since his involvement is quite literally impossible."

"Just a moment while I speak with Keishi. I don't need to convey your threats, do I? Unless he refuses?"

"Whatever it takes, Ito."

Jack waited.

"Come to the station at nine tomorrow morning. You won't need an interpreter; I will be there. Can you bring the witness with you?"

"I haven't met her, but she called Annie after she asked some other English teachers to help her find her. I'll ask Annie to contact her."

"Thank you, Jack. I'm sorry about all this."

"I understand better than you might think. Personal feelings have no place in a murder investigation."

"I appreciate that. See you in the morning."

With that, they both disconnected, and Jack returned to the guest room. Sam and Annie both looked at him.

"Could you call Hannah and ask her if she'll meet me at the police station tomorrow morning at nine? Then could you tell me where it is?"

"I'll call her now, and I can give you a ride in the morning."

"Thanks."

It was Annie's turn to leave the room.

Sam and Jack sat quietly for a moment then both began speaking at once.

They stopped and laughed. "You first," Sam said.

"His boss told him not to speak to me, but when I called his boss, he was told to be present as an interpreter."

Sam nodded. "I guess that answers my question then. He won't want me there."

"No, perhaps you and Annie can get some coffee or something while you wait."

"You always know *just* what to say."

Annie returned with a smile. "She said she'll be there. She sounded a little nervous, but I told her she doesn't have anything to worry about and that you're a medical examiner from the United States."

"Is she Australian?"

"I don't think so. She sounds American."

"What time will we need to leave?"

"Let's shoot for eight thirty. It won't take that long to get there, but we don't want to be late. What do you want to do this afternoon?"

Jack glanced at Sam.

"Can we go shopping in Hamamatsu? I'd like to buy some souvenirs."

"That's fine with me. Jack?"

"Sure. I should probably buy a few things, too. I imagine you know where we can find something interesting."

"I do. In fact, we don't even need to go to Hamamatsu. There are some great gift shops nearby. Afterward, we can eat Japanese pancakes for lunch."

"More pancakes?"

"Don't worry." She grinned at Sam. "They aren't pancakes as you know them; they're savory instead of sweet."

Superintendent Fukuda glared at Ito when he hung up the phone. "I told you not to have any contact with that man."

"I have not. He called you in your office."

"Don't be insubordinate. Why did he call me?"

"Probably because when he requested a meeting with me, I refused."

"If he has a witness, we will have to begin investigating again."

I will have to, you mean. "I have continued investigating because I don't think Akiyama-san is our man."

"Have you made any progress?"

"I received the autopsy report this morning."

"Why haven't I seen it?"

"Please forgive me. I brought it with me, but I'm still trying to decide what it means."

The superintendent held out his hand. He opened the report and scanned it. "This doesn't make sense."

Ito nodded.

"Why would someone strangle a dying man?"

"Maybe they didn't know he was dying? Or maybe we're looking for two different murderers?"

"The poison was in the wooden box?"

"Yes."

"Where did the box come from?"

"I don't know that yet, but it eliminates the need for the poisoner to be close to the victim."

"Well, arrange a simple lineup for tomorrow morning and carry on with your investigation."

Thus dismissed, Minoru went back to his office to ponder the results of the autopsy. *I hope Keishi will allow me to show Jack this report and that he has some useful information.*

Entering the first shop to a chorus of "Itterasshai," Sam went one direction and Jack another. He was amazed by the selection of items, everything from papier-mâché cows with bobbing heads, lacquerware, and ornate handkerchiefs to cast iron teapots and sweatshirts.

"I have no idea what to choose. Help!"

"Who are you shopping for?" Annie asked.

"My personal assistant, a few doctors, maybe a few random gifts for whoever I forgot."

Annie looked around the shop. "The lacquerware is very nice… doctors? Do they have any particular hobbies or interests?"

"One is interested in plants…. one is a foodie, and another collects wooden dolls."

"Lacquerware for the foodie. Does the collector have one like this?"

Jack looked at the tall cylindrical doll with a round head. "I don't know, but it looks interesting to me."

"Then all we need is something for the plant lover. How about a book on bonsai?"

"Do they have one here?"

"I don't think so, but they do at the bookstore. What about your assistant?"

"I don't even know. Maybe I should have bought one of those tea sets Sam bought for her friend."

"We can go back there if you want to. That's where the bookstore is anyway."

"Great. I think I can probably pick out a few random things to add to the collection. What is Sam getting?"

"What isn't Sam getting?" Annie laughed.

"Is she done already?"

"I think so. I left her in line, but she's still looking while she waits. You might find some cute stationary items in the bookstore, too. Oh! We should go to the 100-yen shop. They have all kinds of cool things."

"The mind boggles."

Annie followed Jack to the cash register, talking a mile a minute as he picked up a few additional trinkets.

"I expect Sam is much better at this."

"Better at what?"

"There you are. Better at picking out gifts."

"I really don't know about that. I got Roger a horse with a bobble head." She laughed.

"Those are for good luck. Does Roger like horses?"

"He's my head ranch hand. If he doesn't, he picked the wrong profession."

"Did you get something for Tom?"

"Not yet. I don't know what to get him. Any ideas?"

"Snacks? A Japanese motorcycle? You, back at home?"

Sam sighed as the cashier rang up her purchases.

"Do you even know that many people?" Jack asked.

"I just can't make up my mind."

"We're going to the bookstore and back to the supermarket now. Annie gave me some ideas."

They finished their purchases and drove to the supermarket, where Annie showed them the bookstore, and before long, they had another pile of gifts. "How are we going to get all this stuff home, cuz? We should have brought an extra suitcase. Thank goodness the clothes here don't fit me, or I'd be in real trouble."

<hr>

Once they were finished shopping, Annie took them to an okonomiyaki shop. "I think you'll like this," she said as the server sat them at a table with a grill in the middle. "The batter is like pancake batter and cabbage, but it's not sweet. You can pick any of these things to put in it." Annie pointed at a simple menu card. "Then this sauce, mayonnaise, katsuoboshi, and seaweed powder." She lifted each item.

"What's katsuoboshi?" Sam asked.

"Smoked bonito shavings. They're kind of cool; they move when you put them on the hot okonomiyaki."

"So, they taste fishy?"

"Yes, I guess so."

"Can we get three different ones so we can taste more variations?" Jack asked.

"Sure."

They all wanted bacon, but Annie got squid and shrimp in hers. Sam got ground pork and beni-shoga, a red, pickled ginger. Jack got shrimp and tenkasu, bits of fried tempura to give it a crunch.

When the server returned with their bowls, Annie turned on the gas and showed them how to mix the ingredients, pour them on the grill, and use the spatulas to make them round.

Sam was getting excited, watching them cook. "Isn't it time to turn them over yet?"

"No, not yet. If you try to turn them too soon, they'll fall apart."

After turning them with a spatula on either side, they followed Annie's lead, brushing on sauce and making a zigzag pattern with *Kewpie* mayonnaise. Annie and Jack added katsuoboshi and nori powder, but Sam left them off.

Watching, she said, "Look! They're alive!" when the bonito shavings began to wiggle around on top. "I wish I could've gotten a video of that."

"I'll add some more. Get your phone ready."

Sam's enthusiasm always made Jack smile, and when he cut a piece off his okonomiyaki and took a bite, his smile grew wider. "Itadakimasu," he said belatedly.

"This is so good! Why does this mayonnaise taste different?"

"I'm not sure. It's tangier, I think, but okonomiyaki is definitely not the same with other kinds."

They each tried all of them, and each liked their own choices best. "Everything I try here becomes my favorite, and I want to eat it every day."

"This is high on the list of favorites," Jack said. "Thanks for bringing us here."

"When are we going back to Mos Burger?"

"Maybe tomorrow if Takashi can come home. It's one of his favorites, too."

Chapter 17

nnie parked in front of the police station the next morning at 8:45 and pointed out a young woman who fit Hannah's description, locking up her bicycle. "Would you like us to come inside with you?"

Jack shook his head. "No, I think it would be better if I just enter with the witness. I'll text you when I'm done."

"Thanks, Jack. We'll find something to do until then. Good luck."

They all got out of the car, and Jack headed toward the girl with the blue bicycle. "Hello, I'm Jack, Annie's cousin."

"Hi! Thanks for meeting me here. I'm a little nervous."

"Nothing to be nervous about. Why don't we go inside? I'm not sure how long it will take to find Ito. Do you speak Japanese?" He held the door for her.

"Not much. It's my first year in Japan."

"I don't speak much either, but the inspector speaks very good English."

Jack inquired at the front desk, and the clerk on duty indicated a bench where he assumed they were supposed to wait.

Ito, entering the lobby twenty minutes later, looked at Jack and crossed his arms. "Friend of yours?"

"No, we've just met. I haven't told her anything about your case, other than you need a statement about her whereabouts last Thursday morning."

"Wait here, please, while I take her statement. Come with me."

Ten minutes later, Jack heard a slightly incorrect version of his name being called, and he stood.

A young man with a round face and extremely short hair stood at attention inside the door to the inner sanctum. He bowed as Jack approached and began a litany of Japanese before Jack held up a hand and said, "I'm sorry. I don't speak Japanese."

Non-plussed, the officer turned and led him through the door and down a long hallway, stopping to knock on one of the dozens of doors. He opened the door and ushered Jack inside before stepping back outside and closing it behind him.

Jack took in the scene before him. Ito and an older man with a serious expression sat across a bare wooden table from Hannah. None of them looked happy.

"Explain yourself," Ito said.

"I don't understand."

"Why did you bring this lady here?"

"I didn't. She agreed to meet me here because she said she saw your suspect on the beach Thursday morning."

"Is that true?" he asked Hannah.

"Yes, I think so. I don't know the man I saw, but he was jogging on the beach."

"How do you know it's the same man?"

"Look, I don't know who he was, but I often go to that beach in the morning, and I never see anyone. Last Thursday, I was earlier than usual, and while I was sitting there watching the waves, a man ran by. I remember because I suddenly felt nervous, sitting all alone with no one else around. He looked at me as he ran by, and I decided to leave; then, as I was getting ready to go, he looked back again. I think he was surprised to see me there, too."

"Why didn't you tell me that in the first place?"

"You were talking about this man I knew… I didn't know what you wanted. I've never seen him before or since."

"Do you think you could pick him out of a lineup?"

"I'm not sure. Maybe."

Ito interpreted the conversation for the older man, walked to the door and, spoke to someone outside, then sat back in his chair.

"Foreigners often think all Japanese people look the same. I will be surprised if you can identify him."

"Do his clothes count? I can describe him."

He conversed with the older man for a few moments, then said, "How about this… Jack, step outside the room with me and tell me what he usually wears when he runs. Then, I'll hear her description, and if it's close enough, we will have several men enter the interview room, and she can say yes or no." He took Jack into the hallway. "Are you sure you've never met her before?"

"Positive."

"Okay, how does he dress when he goes jogging?"

"He's pretty noticeable. He wears a headband, and his hair flops up and down on top. He wears a snug t-shirt and running shorts that accentuate his broad chest and short, thin legs. Also, his legs are almost hairless, and he wears white socks and bright orange running shoes."

"You're very observant."

"It's my profession. I imagine you're the same."

"True. Okay. Let's see what our witness can tell us."

They reentered the room, and Ito told Hannah to describe the man on the beach.

She took a deep breath and closed her eyes. "He was far away when I first saw him, and the first thing I noticed was his outline against the sunrise. He looked like a cartoon. You know that one with the dumb blonde guy with the giant head and chest and the tiny hips and legs?"

Jack laughed. "Johnny Bravo?"

Minoru looked at him questioningly, so he pulled up the character on his phone, then Ito chuckled and passed it to the older man, who didn't seem to have a sense of humor.

"What else?"

"As he got closer, I could see his hair bouncing up and down. He had one of those bandanas wrapped around his forehead, under his hair, and his hair was a little long, so…

"I don't know how else to describe it. When he took a step, the hair above his bandana moved, like… like if a child had a doll and was shaking it up and down."

"I think we've got it. Anything else?"

"His face was kind of square and pink from running. His shoes were very bright." Hannah closed her eyes again. "I thought, from the way he looked at me, that he might have wanted to stop and speak to me, but he didn't. That's what made me feel nervous about being alone."

"Did he look mean or scary?"

"No, not at all."

Minoru again interpreted for the other man and waited for his reply. He returned his focus to Hannah. "We will have several people come into the office and say hello. You never heard his voice, right?"

"No, I didn't."

"The men who stop by might have had a haircut and will be wearing different clothes, so you will have to focus on their facial features and body type rather than hair and clothing."

Hannah nodded and sat up straight when the first man entered. "No. Not him. He's too narrow, and his face is too hard."

The second man entered, and Hannah shook her head. "No." When he left, she said, "He has a baby face and is too heavy."

She smiled when the third man entered. "That's him."

Looking startled, Takashi had been forbidden to speak, but when he saw her, he said, "The girl from the beach." He looked at Jack. "You found her."

"Annie found her through the school where she used to work."

"You may return to your cell," Ito told him.

"But…"

"Thank you. Go now."

Jack and Hannah were silent.

"Thank you very much for assisting us with our inquiries. If you will sign a statement, you are free to go. Jack, we would like you to remain."

Jack nodded, then sat quietly while Minoru typed out a statement, and after reading through it to assure its accuracy, Hannah signed it and stood.

After she left the room, Minoru rubbed his eyes. "This is very irregular."

"I know you probably won't be happy with me, but I have interviewed quite a few people and have some information. Is this Keishi Fukuda?"

"Yes, I'm sorry I didn't introduce you earlier."

Jack stood and bowed, proffering his business card. "Olivares Jack desu. Yoroshiku onegaishimasu."

The superintendent nodded solemnly and spoke with Minoru for a moment to get caught up on their conversation.

"Tell us about your interviews, please."

Jack passed the timeline to Minoru and explained how he, Sam, and Annie had traced Minami-san's movements.

Minoru studied the chart before passing it to his boss and interpreting.

"Have you had the box tested?"

"Yes, it contained thallium shavings."

Jack nodded, explaining the box's provenance and how the scarf ended up in Minami-san's possession.

Ito translated for Keishi Fukuda, who looked at Jack with an unfathomable expression, then spoke to Ito in Japanese.

"Anything else?" Minoru asked.

"There's one other thing, but I don't know if it's connected. Someone has been stealing from the Minami pension fund. Mr. Hirano got fired for reporting it."

Ito mulled that over before interpreting for Fukuda.

Interpreting once again, Ito said, "Keishi Fukuda said thank you for coming to us with your information, but you have no authority here and will not interfere any further."

Raising an eyebrow, Jack said, "I understand. May I take Takashi-kun home with me?"

"Yes, he should be discharged by now."

They stood and bowed, Minoru leading him to where Takashi waited and shaking his hand. Under his breath, he said, "I would like to show you the autopsy report. Can we meet at the izakaya tomorrow morning?"

"Of course. Ten-thirty?"

Minoru nodded before turning and walking away.

Pausing on the steps that led from the station, Jack sensed Takashi's deep feeling of relief. He sent Sam a brief text and glanced around as he waited for her reply.

Takashi grabbed the metal rail and swayed weakly.

"When was the last time you ate?"

"I don't remember."

"Have you slept at all?"

"No."

"It's amazing you're still standing." Jack glanced at his phone. "Annie and Sam are on their way. Why don't you sit down while we wait?"

Shaking his head, Takashi stood resolutely, knuckles white in his effort to remain upright. When Annie appeared, running in their direction, Takashi's body began to shake uncontrollably, and his tears flowed unchecked.

Annie flung her arms around him in a fierce embrace and cried with him.

Looking away, Jack's eyes met Sam's. The empathy she projected rocked him to the core. *She has what I'm missing.* He studied her face. *Life is richer, deeper, when she's around.* Wondering for what seemed like the millionth time whether he had made a mistake when he decided not to return to Santo Milagro, he shook his head and approached her. "Are you okay?"

"Yes." Her lips trembled when she smiled. "I'm very happy for them."

Jack realized she was thinking about Tom and their misunderstanding. *Can I sacrifice my happiness for hers? She needs him as much as I need her.*

Annie, after examining Takashi from head to toe, asked if he was up for Mos Burger or just wanted to go home.

"Can we order to go? I want spy-she bah-gah, but not to restaurant."

"You are the king today; we will get them to go. How many?"

"Eight," Sam said.

"Whaaat?"

"Two each, and in case someone like Oba tries to steal one." Sam laughed.

"She might," Takashi nodded. "Better get ten."

Taking his hand, Annie gawped. "You are *all* around the twist."

Chapter 18

By the time the small group arrived home, Annie had called Oba, and the family was waiting in the living room to welcome Takashi home. They weren't demonstrative; there wasn't hugging or crying involved, but Jack observed the happiness in their eyes and felt the decreased tension in the atmosphere. He thought of his father and wondered if he would have shown any emotion had Jack been in a similar situation. Sam, he could see, was shocked.

Takashi didn't say much as they sat around the dining table and shared their burgers. Oba fussed over him, bringing water and snacks to the table and urging him to eat, and Oji talked about how much work he had missed. His grandparents listened to the chatter and studied him quietly, but when there was a lull in the conversation, Obaa-san pointed out the senbazuru hanging above his place at the table and spoke to him in Japanese.

Takashi smiled and thanked her. "It looks like her wish came true."

"We all wished together." Annie took his hand. "I was so worried."

"It was not good. I am happy to home." His eyes closed, and he swayed, nearly falling face-first into his burger, but Annie caught him.

"Jack, can you and Sam help me get him upstairs?"

"Why don't we just lay him in our room for now?"

"Who knows how long he'll be out?"

"That's okay. We'll figure it out later. Somebody might get hurt if we try to navigate the stairs."

Annie nodded and interpreted for the elders, then the three of them carried Takashi's inert form to the guest room. "I'll stay with him for a while in case he wakes up." She sat on the edge of Sam's futon.

"That's fine. Jack and I can take a walk on the beach."

Sam glanced at him, and he murmured in Annie's ear before following Sam out of the room to the entryway.

The beach was devoid of people, as usual, and Sam and Jack sat in the sand and watched the waves roll in. The negative ions soothed Sam as she thought about the Akiyama family and their response to Takashi's return. She wanted to talk about it, but given Jack's upbringing, she didn't know how to broach the subject. Jack, who often seemed to know what she was thinking, brought it up himself.

"I could see you were a little shocked earlier. Do you want to talk about it?"

Brow furrowed, she didn't answer immediately. "I know they care about him, and Oba and Grandma spent so much time folding the cranes, but when he came home, they acted like nothing had happened."

"You could see their affection by the way they focused on him at the table. I think that the visible, emotional response you were expecting would have made everyone uncomfortable."

"Was your mother like that?"

"No. she changed after her many years in America. Takashi is different with Annie, too. Maybe we can ask him about it once he's feeling better."

Sam nodded and stared at the ocean.

"What happened at the police station?"

Jack related what had happened with Hannah and his subsequent interview with Keishi Fukuda. "Minoru asked me to meet with him tomorrow to look at the autopsy report."

"Are you happy about that?"

"Not happy, exactly, but relieved. I won't feel at ease until we've solved the case."

"Always the crow." Sam smiled.

"Finally, back with my cardinal where I belong."

Sam thought about their time in Santo Milagro when she learned about his nickname. His dark eyes, almost black, and his penchant for solving puzzles prompted his peers to call him the crow. He had dubbed her the cardinal because her bright red hair matched their grandmother's painting, which hung on the landing of Sam's ranch house. Birds of a feather, he had said. She had a tattoo of a cardinal and a crow on her back shoulder blade, a souvenir from her time in Las Vegas. *That was probably what he was staring at the other day.* "How long do you suppose Takashi will sleep?"

Jack shrugged. "I have no idea, maybe a couple of days. I don't think he slept at all while he was at the station."

"I wonder if he ate. If not, a Mos burger was probably not a great choice."

"He didn't manage to eat much of it anyway."

"What should we do now? Our room is occupied, and Annie is unavailable."

"Let's take a little trip to Hamamatsu. We can wander around and amuse ourselves and let the family have some privacy."

"Should we take some things this time?"

"No, let's just go. I already told Annie."

Sam elbowed him. "You're so sneaky."

<hr>

They walked to the train station, Jack glancing at his phone now and then, and when they arrived in Hamamatsu, he led her through the station to another platform rather than heading for the exit. "Where are you going?"

"You'll see."

"Are we going somewhere else?"

Jack didn't answer. He stopped as a train approached and scanned the passengers as they exited the train. Sam looked toward the train when Jack grinned, and her breath caught. Tears sprung in her eyes as Tom walked toward them with a small suitcase. She couldn't speak.

He reached them and dropped his bag, gathering Sam into his arms and kissing her forehead. "I'm so sorry, Sam. Can you forgive me?"

Still unable to speak, her pulse racing, she hugged him tightly.

Tom stepped back slightly and took her face in his hands. Her tears flowed freely, and her nose was pink as she gulped air and took a deep breath. "How? Why? Jack?" She didn't take her eyes off Tom.

"Jack called me and told me how worried you were. He bought me a ticket and swore me to secrecy. Say you'll forgive me for being such a jealous jerk when you left."

"I forgive you." Sam sniffed and swiped at her eyes ineffectually. "I'm so glad you're here." She hugged him again and then turned to Jack, whose expression was unreadable. "Thank you, Jack. You are ninja sneaky. I had no idea."

"I got two rooms at the same hotel, so you can catch up in private, but first, let's drop off Tom's bag and visit your favorite izakaya."

Suddenly filled with happiness and eager to show Tom all of the amazing food she had discovered, Sam took his hand and followed Jack through the station with a skip in her step. She still couldn't quite believe he was there and kept wondering when she would wake up. Remembering her dream of the cranes, she turned to him and asked, "When did you and Jack plan all this?"

"Three days ago. It wasn't much time."

"I had a dream." She told him about the senbazuru and her dream.

Tom, used to the flashes of insight she had in her sleep, squeezed her hand and smiled.

Once they had checked into the hotel and dropped off Tom's bag, the three made their way to the izakaya.

Jack ordered beer, and he and Tom let Sam pick out their food before she excused herself to visit the restroom.

Watching her walk away, Tom said, "Thank you, Jack. I know what this cost you."

Jack shrugged. "It's only money."

"I don't mean that kind of cost."

"I know."

The two of them eyed each other from across the table. "I owe you."

"She was miserable. It nearly broke my heart. I guess we're stuck with each other."

"If it's any consolation, I actually like you, Jack. What's more, I respect you, and she'll be much happier with you in her life. She's missed you a lot."

"We'll be one big, happy family." Jack gave a half smile. "It's been good to fix things between us. I'm glad she came."

"I didn't want her to."

"I know. I'm sorry."

"I was jealous. I've never really understood your relationship."

"I didn't help. Here's to Sam." Jack held up his glass. "Kampai."

"Kampai. Here she comes."

Sam rejoined them at the same time the server brought their food, so the remainder of their meal consisted of Sam sharing her favorite izakaya food with Tom, and Jack filling him in about the murder case.

"How are you enjoying Santo Milagro, by the way? Is it enough of a challenge for you?"

Tom glanced at Sam. "It's different."

"You miss the professional stimulation, don't you?" Sam asked.

"I do, sometimes. But I love you, and I enjoy being outdoors and having so many wonderful friends. It's a good life; it's just different."

"You miss the professional stimulation, don't you?" Sam asked.

"I do, sometimes. But I love you, and I enjoy being outdoors and having so many wonderful friends. It's a good life; it's just different."

"That's what worried me when I considered moving there. My work is all I've ever had, and I thought I might end up resenting Sam if I gave it up. I hope I can visit more often, though, if you'll have me."

Smiling brightly, Sam said, "That would make me very happy."

"You're welcome any time," Tom added.

Once their meal was finished and they had returned to the hotel, Jack left Sam and Tom to their own devices. He went to his room, where he took a bath and sat up in bed to deliberate. He pushed thoughts of Sam from his mind and focused on the case. *The basic motives for murder are love, money, and power. Minami-san's wife is said to have hated him, but hate is just the flip side of love, isn't it? His son loves his mother. Could he have killed to protect her? What about the mistress? Did she really love him? Was she involved in the embezzlement? Was she jealous of his wife? And Mr. Watanabe? Was he trying to poison his wife? Or did he know she would give that box to Minami-san? Who else? Could Mr. Hirano be so angry over his dismissal that he killed his boss? Do the housekeeper and the foreman have anything to do with it? Is there anyone we've missed lurking in the background? It's hard to prove anything.*

He fell asleep mid-thought and was awakened by a text notification from Tom at three. *Must be the magic hour.* He texted back and splashed some water on his face.

Opening the door to Tom's knock, he was surprised to see that he held two bottles of Asahi Super-Dry. "Where'd you get those?"

"I got them from a vending machine in Tokyo."

"You were really thinking ahead." Jack grinned. "Why didn't you wake Sam? She would have been more fun than me."

"I know." He laughed. "She just looked so peaceful. I couldn't bring myself to disturb her."

"We were both waking at three when we first got here. Jetlag's a bear." Taking one of the bottles from Tom, he said, "Let's pop this open. We don't have any of those little glasses, though."

"We don't need no stinkin' glasses," Tom drawled.

Jack laughed and opened both bottles, handing one to Tom. "Kampai, buddy."

"Kampai." They clinked bottles. "Why are you dressed?"

"I was laying there puzzling over a list of suspects and fell asleep."

"Did you figure anything out?"

"Not a thing. Hopefully, the autopsy will point at someone."

They drank their beer in silence, and when their bottles were empty, Tom returned to his room, and Jack got ready for bed.

———

They met in the hotel restaurant the next morning and were faced with the decision of what to eat. "At the Akiyama home, we have a choice between fish or toast. What is all this stuff? Even pictures don't help."

"It might be easier to figure out what you want to eat and ask for it," Tom said.

"What do I want?"

"The entire menu, probably."

Sam elbowed Jack. "Coffee, for sure. Maybe eggs and toast?"

"What kind of eggs?"

"I don't care. Whatever they bring me."

"How about you, Jack?"

"That would be fine with me, too."

Tom searched the menu but didn't find what they wanted, so he asked the server in Japanese.

Staring at him as if he had grown a third head, Sam asked, "You speak Japanese?"

"Yes, a little."

"What did you say to the waitress?"

"I asked her if we could get three plates of eggs and bread."

Sam gaped. Then she turned to Jack. "Did you know about this?"

"I did not." One eyebrow rose.

"It would be super funny if she brought us something completely different."

"No, that wouldn't be funny. More like humiliating."

"Did you remember the coffee?"

"She said you can't have any today."

"Liar!"

"No, it's true. Only tea today."

Sam was nearing the edge of her tether when the server arrived with three steaming cups of coffee. She poured cream into her cup and took a sip. "You should be careful," she told Tom. "You could cause an international incident."

"Quit being such a baby," Jack said.

She stuck her tongue out at him and complacently sipped her coffee until their eggs and toast arrived, then she looked at her plate and laughed. "What is this?"

"Well… I'm not sure. We should try it and see."

"Or you could ask."

"Or… no. I don't want to ask." Tom took a bite. "The eggs are those sweet, omelet-type eggs they put in bento boxes, and the bread is just regular bread. Maybe we can make them into sandwiches."

"Weird."

"Drink your coffee. That's what happens when you order something that's not on the menu."

"I want my toast," Sam mock wailed. "Annie, where are you?"

"I can't wait to meet her."

"She's great. I'm going to ask her to come stay with us for a while."

"Should we head back pretty soon?"

"Yes. I wonder if Takashi's awake yet."

"You could text Annie and ask."

"Even if he's still asleep, she could probably use some company. One more coffee first. Will you order one for me, Tom?"

Chapter 19

Inspectors Ito and Mori surprised Harumi Watanabe at home. She answered the door to her second-floor apartment wearing an apron. Ito's stomach rumbled when he smelled toast and coffee.

"Come in," Harumi said. "I've been expecting you."

Scanning her modest demeanor and what he considered very average, middle-aged looks, he wondered what it was about her that would motivate a man like Minami-san to give up everything to be with her. *Or maybe he wouldn't give up everything. He was still married and still retained control of his company.*

"Would you like some coffee?" Her voice startled him.

"No, thank you. We won't take too much of your time."

"Please have a seat." She indicated a well-polished mahogany dining table and took her own coffee to a chair across from him and Mori.

Ito looked around at the spacious, open design of the apartment and the elegant furnishings before focusing his attention on Harumi and asking, "Do you live here alone?"

"Yes. I suppose I'll have to find another place now. This apartment belonged to Yoshinori-san. He moved me here to keep me safe when my husband began hurting me."

"But you didn't seek a divorce."

"No." She looked down and tucked a strand of dull hair behind her ear. "Sometimes I wish I had. He'll think I'll go back to him now."

"We were told that you resigned from your position. Did Minami-san leave you money to live on?"

"No, I don't think so. He thought he was invincible. So did I. He always seemed larger than life."

"Why did you resign?"

"His son never approved of me. I couldn't bear seeing his smiling face behind his father's desk every day. How can he smile?" Harumi's face hardened.

"Can you tell me about the small wooden box he carried with him?"

"A small box with holes in it?"

"Yes."

"My husband gave me that box, and I didn't want it, but it was pretty, and I thought perhaps it would remind Yoshinori-san of me, so I gave it to him as a memento. I thought he would appreciate it, but after I gave it to him, he began distancing himself; he stopped coming here and to the office. I thought he had found someone new." Tears trickled down her cheeks.

"When did you find out he was sick?"

"I didn't."

"I think you did. We discovered your deleted text on his phone. You met with him in the park."

Staring at him with frightened eyes, she said, "I didn't hurt him. I swear I didn't."

"It's okay. I believe you."

"You'll think I killed him. I didn't. He was alive when I left."

"Tell me what happened."

"I found a woman's scarf on his desk." Harumi's voice quivered. "I thought he was seeing someone else, so I insisted that he meet me, and I confronted him. I was so upset that I didn't notice how weak he was. When I flung the scarf at him and demanded to know whose it was, he laughed at me. I thought he was drunk. He put the scarf around his neck and spun in a circle. 'It's mine. Don't I look lovely?' *He laughed.*"

Ito was afraid to interrupt her narrative, so he glanced at Mori, scribbling furiously, but remained silent.

"I was so angry." Harumi was lost in her memories, her eyes staring at nothing. "I slapped his face. If I had done that in the past, he would have grabbed my wrist before my hand made contact. He would have pulled me close and growled at me. But he didn't do that. My hand smacked his cheek and he fell to the ground, then sat there laughing like I wasn't even there. It was terrible. I felt so humiliated, and I stomped away. I swear he was alive and laughing when I left. If only I'd known how sick he was, I would have taken him to the hospital. I didn't get to say goodbye or tell him I loved him."

She was sobbing by the time she finished her story. Ito felt sorry for her but had to continue. "Do you know how he got to the park?"

"Yes, he drove," she answered, gulping air. "I know because his car was parked in front of mine."

"Didn't it seem strange that he drove such a short distance?"

Pausing, she gaped at him. "I didn't think of that."

"Did you see anyone else in or near the park?"

"No. It was very early."

"What time did you meet?"

"At six forty-five. Early because I had to get to work."

Ito stood, followed by Mori, "Thank you for your assistance, Watanabe-san. If you think of anything else, please call." He handed her his business card and bowed.

"I didn't cause his death by not taking him to the hospital, did I?"

"No. Please ease your mind."

Her mouth quivered again as she bowed. "Thank you, Inspector."

Once they were outside, Mori said, "If she had taken him to the hospital, he might have died anyway, but not by strangulation."

"Perhaps. But that's not what she needs to hear."

"Do you believe her?"

"I think so. How about you?"

"Mm. With reservations. What's next?"

"Let's go have a chat with her husband, purveyor of the wooden box."

<hr>

Seated in Minami-san's office, both inspectors stood when Akio entered and introduced Mr. Watanabe. He was a large man, not particularly tall, but wide, with large biceps and a surly demeanor. Akio instructed him to cooperate and left the office, so he sat staring daggers at Ito, perceiving him to be his main interrogator.

"How long have you worked here, Watanabe-san?"

"Fifteen years," he mumbled.

"In the same position?"

"No. I started on the line."

"Do you like your job?"

"It pays the bills."

"Did you like Minami-san?"

Watanabe spit. "Wife-stealer."

"Did you wish him harm?"

After a pause, in which he rearranged himself in his chair, he said, "Only in my heart."

"You work in the laboratory, is that correct?"

"Yes."

"We'd like to ask you about a certain wooden box you gifted your wife."

"What about it?"

"Do you know what she did with the box?"

"Don't know. Don't care."

"What was inside the box?"

Staring fixedly at Ito, he said, "I don't know."

"I think you do. I think you placed thallium shavings inside the box and sealed it shut. Did you wonder why she didn't get sick?"

"I don't know what you are talking about."

"She gave the box to Minami-san, and he became very sick indeed."

Watanabe's ruddy complexion paled, and he sat very still. "I asked her to return the box. That's not what killed him."

"Is that why you strangled him? To make sure he didn't die from the poison?"

"I didn't kill anyone, and you can't prove that I did."

"We can prove intent. We have the box."

"I never. I just wanted to make her a little sick." Watanabe's voice rose with his panic. "I swear I never meant to kill anyone."

"What size shoe do you wear?"

Gaping at him, Watanabe said, "Twenty-nine."

"Measure his shoe for me, please."

Mori pulled out a tape measure and approached.

"Stay away from me, or I'll kick you in the face."

"You'll cooperate if you know what's good for you," Mori said before stooping down and measuring Watanabe's shoe. "It's almost thirty, Keibu."

Ito stood. "Thank you for your time, Watanabe-san. We'll be in touch regarding charges against you."

"I didn't do anything. It was just a prank. I'd never hurt anyone on purpose."

"As I said, we'll be in touch." He and Mori left the office and headed for the exit. "Now, what do you think of that?"

Mori was silent for a moment. "He suffers from stupidity. He's a low life and a wife-beater, but I don't think he actually meant to kill her."

"And his shoe size is wrong." Ito frowned. "Keishi will want an update."

Chapter 20

The Akiyama house felt deserted when Jack and Sam returned with Tom. "Tadaima," Jack called, but there was no answer. Tapping on the guest room doors, Jack slid them open a little and peeked inside, but the room was empty. "What time is it? Did they go out to eat?"

Sam shrugged. "Want me to make some more coffee?"

"Sure. Someone is bound to show up eventually."

"Did you tell Annie that Tom was coming?"

Jack grinned.

"Master of coordination."

Tom was busy looking around. "This is a really interesting house. I like how they've combined the styles to make something new. Did they keep the traditional bath?"

"That's one of my favorite things about this house."

"You're lucky they have this inset table." Tom joined Jack at the dining table. "Traditional Japanese homes and apartments can be hard on the knees. Up and down, up and down. My apartment had a kotatsu and a small sofa without legs and a squat pot."

Setting their coffee on the table, Sam gaped at him, not knowing which question to ask first. "You lived in Japan? How did I not know this?"

Tom shrugged. "I didn't know how to bring it up."

"Where did you live?" Jack asked.

"I lived up north in Morioka for two years."

Sam was shocked. "By yourself? How did you manage?"

"I studied Japanese in college and had a brief homestay while I was waiting for my apartment to be ready.

"Plus, I made friends with my students and the other teachers. It was a great experience."

"Can you describe those things in your apartment?"

"Well, a kotatsu is a small table with a heating element underneath. In the winter, you can put a blanket between the base of the table and the top, then you sit on cushions with your legs under the table, and the heat keeps you warm. I'm sure they have one here, even if they don't use it much."

"That little table in our room is probably a kotatsu, Jack."

"I had to use a portable propane heater in my apartment and leave the window open a crack so I didn't suffocate. I loved the kotatsu, but I had to either sit cross legged or on my knees. Since the sofa was also on the floor, and my futon, of course, I was up and down a lot."

"And the squat pot? What's that?"

Tom laughed. "A traditional-style toilet you have to squat over to do your business. Haven't you seen one?"

The three of them were laughing when Annie and Takashi entered the room. "I'm so sorry. We didn't know when you'd be returning. You must be Tom."

Tom stood and walked toward them. "Yes. Thank you for having me."

"He speaks Japanese!"

"Really? That's great. Obaa-san will be pleased."

"Just a little."

"No, Tom. I speak a little. You can actually communicate," Jack said.

"Do you need something to eat? I don't know where everyone went, but it's about lunch time."

"Can I help you make something? Our breakfast was… not what I was expecting."

"What was it?"

"Tom asked for eggs and bread…"

"Did they give you those sweetie eggs?"

Sam grimaced.

"They are good in bento," Takashi assured her.

"Perhaps, but they aren't too great for breakfast."

"Well, why don't we whip up something tasty for lunch? Takashi, you and Jack could show Tom the bento business."

"Oh-kay. Come on, guys."

The three men left, and Annie turned to Sam with a smile. "You look happy. Was it a big surprise?"

"I couldn't believe my eyes. I cried and cried."

"Why didn't he want you to come to Japan?"

"He and Jack… I don't know. Something happened between them, but they seem okay now."

"Jack's a good friend. I'm glad you're all happy now. What should we make for lunch? Curry?"

"That sounds good. Is it hard to make?"

"It's super easy. They even have boil-in-a-bag instant curry, but it's single serving." Annie pulled out a box and handed it to Sam. "This is the rue. All we need now is a little meat, potatoes, carrots, and onions." She placed the vegetables and a cutting board on the counter. Why don't you cut up the veggies, and I'll cut up the chicken? Then we'll sauté them."

Sam peeled the carrots and potatoes and began to chop. "How's Takashi doing? He looks much better."

"The sleep helped. I think he's still traumatized, but he'll be fine."

"Did you talk to him about the future?"

"No, I couldn't. Maybe after he's gotten over this."

"If you decide not to move, I'd like you to come stay with me for a while, just to relax and look at things from a different perspective. This trip has been great for me."

"I would really like that." Putting the meat into a large pot and distributing it with a spatula, she checked on Sam's progress.

"Don't we need rice?"

"I'll make it as soon as you take over cooking duty." She gave the meat another stir.

Sam added the vegetables and took over at the stove so Annie could make the rice. She watched as Annie measured rice into the cooker and ran water into it. "Don't you have to measure the water?"

"Yes, but you have to wash the rice first." She placed a flat palm into the pot and pressed down as she moved her hand counterclockwise a few times. "You don't want to over-wash it, but you should definitely rinse off any debris." She then placed the side of her hand against the side of the pot and gently poured the water into the sink. "Pay attention to the pan, Sam."

Sam gave the meat and vegetables another stir, then went back to observing Annie. She measured in water and placed the pot in the rice cooker before pushing a button. "It seems like there are a lot of buttons. How do you know which one to push? Mine only has one button."

"This one's fancy schmancy. It has a clock, a timer, and special settings for steaming and reheating. All you need to know about is this green one. It'll be done by the time we're ready to eat."

Peeking into the pot on the stove, Annie retrieved a measuring cup and began to add water. "It should simmer for about twenty minutes, but I secretly let it cook longer so the potatoes begin to disintegrate. They make the rue thicker." Sam giggled at her mischievous, sideways grin.

Once the vegetables were to Annie's liking, she showed Sam how to take the pot off the heat and break the cubes of rue into the pot, stirring until they melted. "Now we put the pan back on the heat and stir it while it simmers and thickens. Then we're ready to eat."

"There's a lot."

"Yes, we'll be able to have it for dinner, too, if you want."

"May I taste it?"

"Sure." Annie pulled out a spoon and handed it to Sam.

"Oh. Gosh. This is delicious. Lunch *and* dinner are fine!"

"Would you like to find the others and tell them lunch is ready? I'll make sure this doesn't stick."

"Can I take some of that rue home with me?"

"We'll pick some up next time we go to the store."

·•·◦◦◦·•·

Entering the bento kitchen, Sam stopped in her tracks and said, "Heyy."

Jack set his glass on the counter and stepped back while Tom hid his behind his back with a grin.

Takashi looked from one to the other and began to chuckle. "Want beer, Sam?"

"Why don't you bring it inside? Lunch is ready."

"What're we having?" Tom asked, kissing her cheek.

"Curry. It's so good. I can't believe we haven't had it before. I am taking some rue home with me."

"If I know we make chicken katsu. Maybe tonight. We go before Annie mad."

"I have a meeting, so I'll see you in a while," Jack said. "Save some curry for me." Sam watched him walk down the street, then followed Tom and Takashi back into the house.

Annie had already set the table by the time they entered, so they sat and picked up their spoons. "Itadakimasu."

"This is delicious. Thank you, Annie."

"And my sous chef, Sam," Annie added.

"I didn't do much, but I learned a lot."

"Tadaima," came a chorus of voices from the entry.

"Okaerinasai."

"Uh oh. Your mom caught me," Annie glanced at Takashi from the corner of her eye. "I'm in trouble now."

The senior members of the household entered the living area, and Tom and Annie stood.

165

Etsuko frowned at Annie, who began explaining in Japanese and diverted the conversation by introducing Tom.

"Hajimemashite." He bowed. "Cork Tom desu. Sam no tsureai. Yoroshiku onegaishimasu."

"Ehhh. Ninhongo wo hanasemasuka?"

"Sukoshi dake," Tom humbly denied his speaking ability, then bent to retrieve his bag. "Douzo. Chisai na omiyage motte kimashita." He bowed again and offered Oba and Grandma gifts. "Nani mo nai kedo. New Mexico no tabemono to Sam-chan no bizcochito cookies desu."

"You made bizcochitos?"

"I did. I thought you might like some, too."

"What else did you bring?"

"Jerky, tortilla chips, two kinds of salsa, and piñon brittle."

The family opened Tom's gifts and discussed them at length before Etsuko turned to Annie and revisited the curry. Seeming appeased at her explanation, she tried the jerky and the brittle.

"We could make some burritos to eat with the chips and salsa if we could find some refried beans," Sam said.

"We could take the shinkansen to Nagoya tomorrow. There's a big import store there, and you might like to see the city?"

"Have you been there before, Tom?" Sam asked.

"No. I've never been farther south than Mt. Fuji. I noticed we can see it from here."

"I wish we had time to climb it while you're here. The sunrise is spectacular."

"Maybe next time." Tom winked at Sam.

⁓⬥⁓

Watching Jack enter the izakaya from his regular table, Minoru was glad to see him. Keishi Fukuda had not said he could meet with Jack, but he had a small out if he was confronted since his superior had met with the man the day before. *Hopefully, he won't find out.* He stood and bowed as Jack approached the table.

"Thanks for coming. I brought that for you to look at." He nodded at the report sitting on the table.

Jack sat down and picked up the folder. He understood Minoru was going out on a limb, letting him see it. "Have you eaten?"

"No, but I ordered a few things." He poured beer into Jack's glass, then his own, as Jack opened the folder. The report itself was in Japanese, but the technical findings were in English and accompanied by numerical data. Scanning the numbers, Jack's eyebrow rose. "What I really wondered was if he died of the poisoning or the strangling. I had guessed thallium because of the symptoms and because it doesn't need to be ingested. It's amazing he could get up out of bed, let alone make it to the park with thallium levels that high. He was very near death. Have you checked his phone for a call or message that morning?"

"The tech department found a deleted text from a contact called 'office' asking him to meet in the park. The sender said it was urgent."

"Have you traced the number?"

"It was from his secretary's phone."

"So, an urgent text from his mistress got him up from his death bed and over to the park. Did he walk there? It's not far, but that doesn't seem possible in his condition."

Minoru related his interviews with the Watanabes and then said, "Someone was watching them, I think. I found a footprint behind a nearby tree."

"How would that person know he would be there? And would they be able to take his keys and drive his car home? Maybe Harumi's husband? Since he gave her the box, maybe he wanted to get it back and covered up the poisoning with the strangling?"

"His feet are the wrong size. Besides, what would he do with his own car? He doesn't live in the neighborhood." Ito shook his head. "What am I missing?"

"Perhaps you can check all the suspects' shoe sizes. It's unlikely that the killer is someone you haven't interviewed, isn't it?

"Have you checked his car for prints?"

"We just confirmed that he drove to the park and have dusted for prints. A second set overlaps Minami-san's on the door and the steering wheel, but we haven't found a match."

"Where were the keys?"

The glass Minoru was raising stopped mid-air. "That's a good point. The car was unlocked, so we didn't need them, but if they're inside the house... I wonder."

Jack's grandmother loved Tom, and he sat on the floor in front of the sofa for hours, listening to stories about Jack's mother. She had been a lively child and often in trouble in high school because she had a mind of her own and didn't always follow the rules. Her English teacher suggested that she be allowed to do a foreign exchange her senior year, and Obaa-san, at her wit's end, decided that it was a good solution.

After spending a year in central California, in a town called Manteca, Sachiko was hooked. She returned to California for college, only returning home during summer vacations.

Tom asked a lot of questions, and when Obaa-san reached the part about her daughter's marriage, she paused. "Did Jack tell you about his father?"

"Yes. Do you know who he was?"

"No, she never told me. She seemed very happy with the man who became her husband, but I always worried that she didn't tell him."

"He found out on the day she died. Jack didn't have a very happy childhood."

Nodding, Obaa-san's eyes looked sad. "Poor boy. I wish we could have spent time with him. His father wrote to us after Sachiko's death, but he never told us their address or answered our letters. I can't speak English, but I hope you'll tell him about his mother. She was a lovely girl."

"I'll tell him. I'm glad I got to meet you Akiyama-san."

"Obaa-san de ii." Her face crinkled in a smile.

Tom smiled back. *She must have had a happy life with all those creases. The perfect grandmother.*

The Akiyama household and guests, having reached nine members, became something of a challenge. Annie added an extra futon in the guest room and made the giant pot of curry, but they still had to negotiate bath times. She felt grateful that Tom spoke Japanese and didn't have to be oriented to the household. He and Obaa-san seemed to get along well, and he managed to include Ojii-san in their conversation as well. They asked him many questions about his work and New Mexico.

As dinner progressed, Annie turned to Sam and said, "Since Takashi and Tom got plenty of rest last night, maybe we should go out for a while and let the rest of the family relax and take their baths. What do you think?"

"Sounds good to me. What do you guys think?"

Jack nodded his assent, and Tom looked over from his place across the table with a smile. "It might be a good idea to give them a break."

Sam observed Jack's smiling grandparents and said, "I haven't seen them so happy since we got here."

Frowning as he glanced in Tom's direction, Jack turned his attention to Takashi and changed the subject.

Annie excused herself from the table and went upstairs, where she called Keiko and asked her if she could go out with them. After they made plans to meet, she sat on her bed and thought about their guests. She liked Tom, but she saw that his presence changed everything for Jack. *He invited him to make Sam happy, but this is supposed to be his family visit. I don't want him to leave feeling like it didn't go well.*

She returned to the table and found it much as she had left it. "Is everyone ready for dessert?"

"Absolutely," Sam said, clapping happily. "Can I help you serve?"

"Nope. You know the rules. I'll be right back."

Oba stayed at the table and let Annie serve for once.

Chapter 21

On their way to the bar, Annie put her arm through Sam's and hung back a little. Keiko had met them outside and was asking Takashi about his recent experience. She seemed to be doing an excellent job of including all three men in the conversation. Unsure of how to broach the subject, Annie leaned into Sam and said, "Would you tell me about whatever is going on between Jack and Tom?"

Sam glanced at her in surprise. "Is it that obvious?"

Nodding, Annie looked ahead at the little group in front of them. "I can see that Jack's trying hard, but he's unhappy. It almost seems like he's jealous, but he's your cousin, right?"

"He is, and he isn't. We found out that his mother was pregnant with him before she married my uncle and that we're not related by blood. I love him dearly and need him in my life, but he and Tom..."

Understanding dawned on Annie, and her admiration of Jack's selflessness grew. "You understand what it took for him to fly Tom over here, right?"

"He was just being nice."

How can she be so blind? "Sam, he's suffering. He gave up his precious time with you, and Tom, even though he seems like a great guy, is even spending quality time with Obaa-san. He's been talking to her for hours like Jack wishes he could. At the table, when you said you hadn't seen her so happy, he felt it like a knife. I could see it in his face."

"I can't seem to do anything right," Sam muttered.

"I don't think it's your fault, but I'd hate for Jack to go home feeling bad about this trip.

"That's why I invited Keiko tonight; I didn't want him to feel like a fifth wheel."

"I'll talk to Tom and make sure we don't leave Jack out. Thank you."

"I'm pretty sure Tom knows exactly how Jack feels."

Sam pursed her lips. "If I spend more time with Jack without saying anything to Tom, then the pendulum will swing in the other direction."

They had reached the bar and joined the others at the door. "Were you two hatching plans back there?" Tom put his arm around Sam's shoulders.

"Maybe," she teased.

Annie observed Jack watching Sam. He schooled his features into an unreadable mask and turned to Keiko. "Shall we?" he asked, opening the door for her. *There's really no good solution. I hope the three of them can work it out.*

Jack pulled out a chair for Keiko and engaged her in conversation. She was a beautiful young woman, but they didn't have much to talk about. "What kind of work do you do?"

"I'm an office lady."

He figured she meant secretary but wasn't sure. "For what kind of company?"

"I work for Yamaha. We make musical instruments." She gazed at him and played with her long hair.

"Do you have any hobbies?"

"I study English."

"You speak very well."

"Thank you." She smiled.

"Do you use English at work?"

"No."

This is like pulling teeth. "Do you like to travel?"

"Someday, I hope I can visit Australia with Annie."

Sam sat quietly, sipping her drink and listening to the conversations swirling around her. Akio, also silent, had shown up and sat to her right. He kept an eye on Jack and Keiko and drank steadily. "How's it going at the factory?" Sam finally asked. "Are you enjoying being the big boss?"

"I thought my father wasn't doing anything, but I was wrong. He had many responsibilities that I didn't know about. I've been very busy. The police don't help. They keep coming around and interrupting. Watanabe-san got so upset she quit, and now I don't have a secretary."

"That must be terrible. She probably knew a lot about your father's job."

"I have asked her to come back and offered her more money, but she said no. I don't know what to do now."

"Have the police found any new evidence?"

His shoulders slumped. "I don't know. They made an appointment to interview us at home tomorrow, so maybe I'll hear something. I should go." When he stood unsteadily and staggered toward the door, Keiko excused herself and caught up with him, taking his elbow.

That's interesting. Tom was involved in a lively discussion with Takashi and Annie, so Sam moved to the empty seat next to Jack. "Want to do a karaoke encore, cuz?"

"No, that was a one-time event." He grinned.

Sam took a deep breath. "Do you regret bringing Tom here?"

"Now, why would you think that?" His eyes glittered.

"It's changed our dynamic."

"But you're happier."

"I'm relieved to know that he's okay and that we're okay, but I was enjoying hanging out with you, just the two of us."

"I was too. Can we send him home now?"

She could see that he was only half joking. "I have a feeling he wouldn't take that too well, but maybe I can have a word with him."

"About what?" Jack held her gaze.

"We can't just leave him home when we go somewhere."

"I don't know. I'll have to think about it."

"What did Akio have to say? He was sloshed when he left."

"The police have been at the factory, and his secretary quit. He's pretty stressed out. He said he and his mom have an interview tomorrow, and he hopes they'll find out what's going on."

"It's hard being on the outside looking in. I haven't been in this situation before. I want to jump in and take charge, which is exactly what the superintendent expects."

"Will you meet with Inspector Ito again?"

"I hope so. Not knowing what happened will give me nightmares."

Tom stood and walked to the stage, scanning the directory. He made his selection and took up the microphone. The traditional music of Japanese Enka began, and Tom began to sing Yosaku. All the patrons in the bar stopped what they were doing and stared. Some of them cheered, and others gaped as this tall, foreign man sang a song that no foreigner should even have heard of.

Takashi watched Tom in awe. "How does he know *Yosaku*?"

"Someone must have taught him." Annie laughed.

Sam and Jack also watched Tom's performance.

"He's trying to regain your attention," Jack said.

"Why does he feel so threatened by you?"

Jack shrugged. "You would have to ask *him* that."

After Tom sang, he approached Jack and put his hand on his shoulder. Leaning over, he spoke in Jack's ear. "Can we go outside and have a private conversation?"

Jack's eyebrow rose, but he nodded and told Sam they would be right back, then followed Tom outside.

———————— ·•·⇐∞⇒·•· ————————

When they had walked several yards away from the entrance, Tom stopped and turned toward Jack. "We need to clear the air. You brought me here, but it's obvious that you wish you hadn't.

"Is it because you're still in love with Sam?"

"No. You don't really understand about Sam and me. We don't have that kind of relationship. We never have."

Tom frowned and rubbed his chin. "The last time we spoke, you told me I should leave her and let you pick up the pieces."

"I was joking."

"No, you weren't. I could see it in your eyes. Why do you want me out of the picture if you're not in love with her?"

"I wish I'd brought my drink with me."

"Here." Tom pulled a flask from his pocket and handed it to him.

Taking a swig, Jack handed it back and cleared his throat. "When I met Sam…" He paused. "My life was very empty. It still is. But when I'm with her, I suddenly see things through her eyes. Everything around me is new and exciting. I feel joy and love—real happiness. And when she's gone, it all disappears again." Jack closed his eyes for a moment. "My life might have been different if Ally hadn't died. Did Sam tell you about her?"

"I've heard her name."

Jack nodded. "Preciosa was her kitten."

"So, you want to be with Sam because she makes you feel alive, but you want her to be alone when you're in Albuquerque?"

"I sound very selfish when you put it that way."

"Aren't you? What do I have to do with the way Sam makes you feel?"

"You take over. Everything." Not one to express his feelings, Jack wasn't sure where that came from, but once he started, he couldn't seem to stop. "When you're around, she's busy worrying about you. She doesn't share her thoughts with me. It's like she forgets I'm there. And now you've shown up here and taken over my family visit. This evening, Sam said she hasn't seen Grandma looking so happy since we arrived. That's because of you. You, sitting with her and hearing stories about *my* mother. I'm here to meet my family, and there you are, standing center stage.

"I feel like I might as well go home now."

Tom gaped at him. He opened his mouth to speak and then shut it again, staring silently. "I… god, Jack, I had no idea. I don't know what to say except I'm sorry. I think I've really misjudged you."

"Sam is an angel sent to help me battle my demons. I need her in a way you'll never understand."

"I don't need to understand. I've just been jealous because I know she loves you, and I thought you meant to steal her away from me. Let's start over. Please? I'll do better. I'll give you time with Sam, and I can help you talk to your Grandmother. I've just been a poor substitute."

Jack saw the pleading in Tom's eyes and was tempted by his offer, but his distrust ran deep. "Flask," he said, reaching out a hand.

He took a swig. "How did you misjudge me, other than thinking I was trying to steal your wife?"

"I thought you didn't care about anyone except yourself. You always seem so cool and self-possessed, like nothing can touch you. I could never understand why Sam cares about you so much because you hurt her over and over again when you didn't respond to her invitations."

"I didn't want to see her. It was too painful. I thought it would be easier to just forget her."

"But you couldn't."

"It's been like trying to cut out my own heart."

"Can we try again?"

Jack nodded and held out his hand. Tom grasped it in his and pulled him in for a brief hug, patting him briskly on the back so it wouldn't get weird. "Let's go back inside. Is that flask empty yet?"

"Not quite. Next time, bring a bigger one." Jack handed it back and gave him a minuscule smile.

⁘

Upon reentering the bar, Jack returned to his seat next to Sam, and Tom invited Takashi to sing with him. Sam glanced at Jack.

"Is everything okay between you two?"

"I think so." He watched Tom on stage, wondering if he had meant what he said. "Have you been having a good time?"

"Not really. I've been worrying about the two of you." She scanned his face. "No blood or bruising… so you talked?"

"Yes. He's a talker."

"It helps sometimes. Most of us don't have ESP."

Jack chuckled and poured himself another drink.

"That was a hint. Do you want to tell me what you talked about?"

"No, once was enough. I'm all talked out."

"Okay. Pour me one, too." She held out her glass. *I guess I'll have to find out from Tom.* She watched him hamming it up with Takashi and smiled. *He's a good man.*

Tom took Jack's seat when he returned to the table, and Jack accompanied Annie onto the small stage. Tom leaned toward Sam and kissed her cheek.

"You're in a good mood. What did you and Jack talk about?"

"He didn't tell you?"

She shook her head.

"He told me I take over when I'm around, and I promised to do better."

She scrunched up her face. "How are you going to do that?"

"I'm not sure. But one thing I *can* do is help him talk to Obaa-san."

"Have I told you lately how much I love you?"

Tom took her hand. "I love you too, Sam, and I want you to be happy."

Leaning her head against his shoulder, she smiled and watched Jack and Annie finish their song.

Chapter 22

Ito and Mori pulled up in front of the Minami house at nine o'clock and parked the cruiser. They had discussed the case in detail after their interview with Watanabe-san and decided to question the widow and her son together. Akio responded to their knock and led them to the sitting room across the hall, where his mother was seated at the kotatsu with a pot of tea.

Both detectives bowed, and Ito said, "Please don't get up."

Kazue nodded and invited them to sit before pouring their tea. "Do you want Akio-kun to stay?"

"Yes, please. We have discovered that your husband was being poisoned before his death," Ito began.

"But that is not what killed him, right?" Akio asked.

"No, it is not, but it has been puzzling us. We have been wondering why someone would strangle a man who was already on the verge of death. Why not just let him die of the poisoning? Can you think of a reason for that?"

Akio shifted his weight and glanced at his mother.

"Would you like to hear how he was being poisoned?"

"Yes," Kazue said at the same time her son said, "No."

Mori looked up from his notes.

"Why aren't you interested Minami-san?" Ito asked Akio.

"It's irrelevant since he died of strangulation."

"Perhaps, but I will tell you anyway." He noticed the tension in Akio's shoulders. "Your father was gifted a small wooden box. It was a curious item because it was glued shut and had small holes drilled into it. When we tested the box, it was found to contain thallium shavings. Do you know what thallium is, Minami-san?"

Keibu Ito looked directly into Akio's eyes, which, interestingly, showed relief rather than fear.

"Yes, it's a soft metal we use at the factory."

"You understand its toxicity?"

"Yes. We keep it stored securely in a safe environment."

"Who has access to the thallium?"

"My father and I did, the foreman and several men who work in the laboratory."

"The box in question was given to Watanabe Harumi by her husband, who works in the laboratory, I understand."

"Was she trying to kill him?"

"No, her husband was trying to kill her, but she didn't want his gift and gave it to your father as a memento."

Kazue covered her smile with her right hand. "His mistress accidentally poisoned him?"

Keibu nodded and stared at Akio. "What size shoe do you wear?"

"Twenty-seven. Why?"

"Someone was at the park observing your father's meeting with Watanabe Harumi-san the morning of his death. She told us about their meeting and the scarf."

"What about the scarf?"

"You left it on your father's desk, and Watanabe-san saw it. Since he had been absent a lot, she thought he had started seeing someone else. She sent him an urgent text to meet her in the park, and when he arrived, she confronted him with the scarf."

"What scarf is this?" Kazue asked.

"Akiyama-san's scarf, the one you asked your son to return."

Kazue looked at Akio. "Why didn't you return it?"

"I forgot it on father's desk."

"When confronted by Watanabe-san, your father laughed and, in a rage, she slapped his face and stormed out of the park. The next day, she heard he was dead."

Kazue's mouth fell open, but Akio remained rigid, his face shuttered.

"We've been wondering how your father, in a very weakened state, could have walked all the way to the park, but he didn't walk, did he?"

"How would I know?"

"You know because you drove his car home after you killed him."

"You can't prove that."

"His car was seen at the park. Where are the keys?"

"They are in their usual place," Kazue said. "In the basket by the door."

Ito stared at Akio. "Are the fingerprints on the steering wheel yours?"

"Why would I kill my own father?"

"Why don't you tell me?"

"Akio-kun?"

"Don't listen to him, mother. He's wrong, just like he was wrong about Takashi-kun."

"You were trying to protect your mother, weren't you? You thought she was poisoning your father, so he had to die from something else before he died from the poison. It was so easy, wasn't it? The scarf was already around his neck, and he was so weak."

"You thought I would poison him?"

"You joked about it before. He said you were."

Kazue looked down in shame.

"We will wait here while Keibu-ho Mori searches for the shoes that match the cast we took, and then I would like you to come to the station with us for voluntary questioning."

"No, I know what that means. I won't go."

"If you don't come voluntarily, we will seek an arrest warrant."

"You do that. I'm innocent, and I'm not going anywhere with you."

Mori left the room, and Akio tried to follow him, but Ito told him to sit down.

When Mori returned with the matching shoes, Ito formally arrested Akio and led him outside to the cruiser. Kazue didn't look at them as they left. She remained sitting at the kotatsu.

Oji entered the house and said, "Akio-kun has been arrested."

"How do you know?"

"I just saw the police take him in handcuffs."

Annie stared with wide eyes, and Takashi muttered under his breath, causing her to start. "We have to go see Kazue-san."

"What's happened?" Sam asked.

"They've arrested Akio. Come on."

Annie left the house and ran across the street, Sam right behind her. She knocked on the door, but no one answered. She knocked again, then opened the door. "Kazue-san, it's Annie. Can I come in?" She stepped inside. "Kazue-san daijoubu desu ka?" Sliding the paper doors open across the hall, she saw Mrs. Minami sitting before the kotatsu, staring at nothing. She looked up at Annie with a blank face. "My life has ended."

Rushing to her side, Annie knelt and placed her hand over Kazue's. "What can we do? Won't you come over and stay with us while he's gone?"

"I want to die."

"No, Kazue-san. Please. Come with me." Annie's heart pounded in her chest. "They took Takashi-kun in first. Remember how worried we were? But he came home. Everything will be okay."

"I think I'll lie down and rest. Perhaps you can help me to my room."

Once she saw that Kazue was comfortable, she returned to the sitting room. "I'm very worried, Sam. I don't know what to do."

"She won't actually try to kill herself, will she?"

"I don't know. We should ask Etsuko-san. She'll know what to do."

When they returned, Jack and Tom were sitting at the table with coffee. All eyes were on Annie.

"How is she?" Jack asked.

She shook her head and addressed her mother-in-law in Japanese. Etsuko remained silent for a few minutes, then joined them at the table. "Kazue-san is very proud. I don't know if she is strong enough to withstand this."

"What can we do?"

"I ask myself, what would I do if Takashi-kun killed his father and was taken to jail? How deeply would I feel that grief and shame? Could I survive that?"

"You would still have Ba-ba and Ji-ji and me. Kazue-san is alone. Does she have other family?"

"I haven't heard of any." She stood and went into the kitchen.

Annie interpreted.

"Is it the shame or the grief that makes her want to give up?" Sam asked.

"Probably both. Yoshinori-san brought shame on the family, but she still had her son."

Sam thought about Oba's response and Annie's words. *How would I feel in that situation? Would I just give up?*

"Where's Takashi?" Jack asked.

"He and his father went to speak with Shima-san."

Jack's grandparents entered the living room as two voices called, "Tadaima."

"Okaeri," the others intoned.

"Gohan." Etsuko and Annie began setting the table as everyone settled in their spots.

The meal was a silent one. Everyone ruminated over their own private thoughts and was likely relieved when lunch was over. Jack announced that he had a meeting with Ito. Annie and Takashi said they were going for a walk, so Sam and Tom enjoyed some private time.

183

Annie had finally decided to broach the subject of returning to Australia. Although she knew Takashi loved her, she also knew he was not very perceptive and couldn't guess her feelings. She had to spell it out for him. She was nervously contemplating how to begin when he took her hand and said, "You wanted to talk to me before I went to the police station."

"Yes."

"You've been unhappy. I was thinking about your words the whole time I was there, worrying that I wouldn't have the chance to fix things. What should I do?"

"Sam suggested maybe we could move to Australia for a couple of years. You could learn more about business, and we could refresh our relationship."

Takashi swallowed. "I don't think we can do that."

Annie stopped and removed her hand from his. They had walked to the beach, and she could feel the sand in her shoes. Looking out at the water, she imagined going under and not having the strength to push her way to the surface. Her panic rose until, taking great gulps of air, she fell to her knees, hyperventilating.

Takashi fell to his knees, facing her, and took her chin in his hand. "Annie. Look at me. Slow your breathing. Breathe in one, two. Breathe out one, two. Look into my eyes and breathe with me."

Gradually, her breathing slowed, and tears rolled down her cheeks. "I can't."

"Isn't there any other way? I am afraid if I send you to Australia by yourself, you won't come back to me." He took her hand again. "Please don't leave me, Annie," he whispered.

"Sam said I could visit her ranch. Could you come with me part of the time? You never take a vacation."

"Do you think that will help?"

"Maybe. I hope so."

"Then that's what we will do. Just don't leave me. I love you so much." He put his arms around her and leaned his forehead against hers.

Chapter 23

Instead of meeting him at the izakaya, Minoru invited Jack to his apartment. He gathered that this was unusual and felt honored by Minoru's trust. He asked Oba to call for a taxi and showed the driver the text with the address.

Minoru met him downstairs and ushered him to his apartment on the fourth floor. "I'm sorry it's not much, but I wanted to speak privately. Please come in."

Removing their shoes in a small entryway, Minoru led Jack into a large, combined kitchen and dining room. He pointed to a short hallway on the left, where Jack could see a washing machine and two doors. "The toilet is on the right and the bath on the left."

Walking through the dining room, they entered a tatami room with a television, a kotatsu, and a bookshelf. On the far side, sliding glass doors led to a small balcony. "This is the living room," Minoru said, and opening sliding paper doors on the left, he continued, "and this is my bedroom."

Jack looked around. He saw a heavy, wooden wardrobe and another television. "Where is your bed?"

"In here." Minoru opened another set of sliding doors to show Jack a neatly folded futon.

In fact, everything is very neat. Not one thing out of place. Jack was impressed. "This is great. You've managed to make it very comfortable and homey without any clutter. If I lived here, I'd want an apartment just like this one."

"I know it isn't much, not like American apartments."

"I love it. It's much bigger than I imagined."

"You should see some of the apartments in Tokyo.

"Some are about half the size of my living room and four times as expensive. Are you hungry? I bought bento lunches and beer."

"Are you off today?"

"Yes and no. I have paperwork, but we have a confession. I'll tell you about it over lunch. Go ahead and have a seat."

They sat at the rectangular table and Minoru poured them each a glass of beer, considerably larger than the thimble-sized ones at the pub. Then they opened their bento boxes, and Jack paused to admire the food inside. "I'm always amazed at the presentation. Japanese food is like art."

"Yes, art. That is the goal. Food should arouse all the senses, how it looks, the texture, and the taste. I am glad you can appreciate it. Not everyone does."

One compartment contained rice sprinkled with black sesame seeds. A sour plum adorned the middle, and a leaf perched in one corner. Perfectly grilled teriyaki chicken, cut into bite-sized strips, sat in a smaller compartment, and shredded salad in a third. For dessert, a light-pink rice cake filled with sweet red beans sat wrapped in a green leaf.

"Itadakimasu. Do you like umeboshi?" Minoru picked up the sour plum with his chopsticks and popped it into his mouth. "The cherry tree leaf is edible, by the way. You can eat it with the mochi if you want to."

"Itadakimasu." Jack picked up his plumb and put it in his mouth as well, then grimaced. It was extremely sour and very salty, and he had to chew around the seed.

"Try it with some rice," Minoru suggested. "I suppose it's an acquired taste."

Jack added rice and then, after disposing of the seed, took a swig of beer. "Wow. That was unexpected."

"The look on your face was so funny. Want another? I have some in the fridge."

"No, that's okay. I think I'll move on to the chicken."

Minoru laughed, then became serious.

"I wanted to ask you something. Do you think it might be possible for me to become a detective in the United States? Maybe somewhere with a lot of Japanese visitors, like Las Vegas?"

"What did you study at university?"

"Criminal Justice."

Jack sat back and considered the question. "I'm not a policeman, but I think you would qualify with your education and experience. The person you should talk to is Sam's husband, Tom. He's a detective and used to work in Las Vegas."

"Is he here in Japan?"

"Yes. I'll text and see if they can come over. That way, Tom can hear about the case and maybe give you a recommendation." He sent Sam a text and poured some more beer.

As they bit into the soft, chewy mochi, Jack's phone pinged. He saw Sam's text and smiled. "They'll be here soon."

"Thank you. I'm excited to meet him."

Jack texted them the address, and Minoru poured more beer.

"Don't get drunk first." Jack laughed.

Unsure of what to expect, Minoru's heart was thumping when he answered the door. Sam was as he remembered, and standing by her side was a tall man with bright blue eyes and a kind face. To Minoru's surprise, he bowed and said, "Hajimemashite. Cork Tom desu. Ojamashimasu."

"Ehh. Subarashii. You speak Japanese very well."

Tom smiled. "No, just a little. Sam told me you speak perfect English."

"You're too kind. Please come in. Would you like some beer and snacks?"

"Of course they would," Jack said from the table. "What have you kids been up to?"

Tom smiled, and Sam blushed.

"Never mind. Forget I asked.

"Minoru was about to tell me how he wrapped up the case, and I thought you might like to hear."

"Yes to beer. Yes to snacks. Yes, to how you wrapped up the case." Sam plopped down in one of the kitchen chairs with her usual enthusiasm. "Do you have some of those round sembei crackers with the cheese spread in the middle?"

"Cheese okaki?"

"Yes! Those are my favorite."

"Sorry. I don't have any, but I'll remember for next time." He brought out some soy sauce-flavored crackers, peanuts, and Pocky sticks for them to snack on, then sat down and poured beer for everyone.

"Okay. Let's hear it. The last time I spoke with you was after your interviews with the Watanabes."

"Right. I was frustrated because Mr. Watanabe's shoe size wasn't a match."

"What made you suspect Akio?"

"It was partially a process of elimination, but Mrs. Minami and the housekeeper both mentioned that Mr. Minami accused his wife of poisoning him. We were trying to figure out why someone would strangle a dying man."

"And if Akio believed that his mother was poisoning his father, he would want to protect her." Jack nodded.

"Minami-san drove his car to the park, but it was at home after he died, and his keys were in the house. We found fingerprints on the steering wheel but didn't know who they belonged to. Mori and I went to the Minami home yesterday morning and interviewed mother and son together. It was evident that Akio thought his mother was poisoning his father and was relieved to hear about the wooden box. His mother was appalled." He glanced at Jack. "I asked him to come in for voluntary questioning, but he refused. So, I sat with him while Mori searched for the shoe that matched the footprint in the park, then I arrested him.

"Technically, we are supposed to have a warrant, but under the circumstances, I applied for one when we arrived at the station."

"And he confessed?"

"Yes. After we took his fingerprints, showed him the cast of his footprint, and laid out the evidence, he broke down and told us everything."

"Was protecting his mother his only motive?" Jack asked.

"He was angry with his father for dishonoring the family, but he told us that he did it to protect his mother."

Breaking the silence a moment later, Tom said, "That was some fine investigative work, Inspector."

"Thank you. I appreciated Jack's help."

Jack poured another round of beer and addressed Tom. "The reason I asked you here, "Is because I wanted you to meet Minoru. He studied Criminal Justice in Texas and is interested in working in the United States. He mentioned Las Vegas, so I thought you might have some advice."

Tom considered that. "Any particular reason you were thinking about Las Vegas?"

"I thought I would be most useful in a city with a lot of Japanese residents or visitors."

"You might consider taking a vacation or a leave of absence and checking out law enforcement in a small town and then applying for positions in areas you might like. The Dallas area has a fairly large Japanese population, for example."

"You don't think Las Vegas is a good place to work?"

"Have you been there?"

"No."

Sam leaned forward. "I met Tom in Las Vegas. I'm from a small town where we live now, and I found Las Vegas very disorienting. The neon lights, the crowds of people, and the constant noise. The only time I could relax was when I was locked in my hotel room."

"With the high concentration of people, the gambling, the drinking, comes a commensurate amount of violent crime.

"I was addicted to my work before I met Sam. It was my life, but if you want to enjoy your life a little, you might want to keep your options open."

"Do you think I could get a job in a regular city?"

"How were your grades in college?"

"Mostly Bs."

"And how long have you been a policeman?"

"Ten years. I've been a detective for six of those."

"I think you're more than qualified. Why don't you come visit Santo Milagro and then I can take you to Vegas and introduce you around if you like?"

"Santo Milagro is where you work now?"

"Yes. It's a very nice little town where everyone knows each other."

"We've had some murders in our 'nice little town'," Sam added.

Minoru wasn't surprised. *Murder can happen anywhere.* "What happened?"

"When Jack and I first met, we bonded over a double murder."

"Sam got kidnapped."

"Wait a minute. Why haven't I heard about this?" Tom complained.

"You know how she is. She got involved in your case in Vegas."

"That's true." He mulled that over.

"And you took an arrow for her up on the mountain."

The more he heard, the more curious Minoru became. "Are you a private investigator?"

Sam smiled wanly. "Not even close."

"She's a murder magnet." Jack laughed.

"It's not really funny." Tom's brow furrowed. "I worry."

"What about the arrow on the mountain?"

"Sam runs a survival school, and she held her first camp in the mountains. We got snowed in, and a killer with a bow and arrows wanted to shut it down."

"That was scary."

"How big is Santo Milagro?"

"The town itself is very small, only a few blocks. But it's surrounded by miles of ranchland. I'd guess there are around two thousand residents."

"And you work as a detective in such a small town?"

"The sheriff's office is also small, so I share duties when we don't have any active investigations. They kind of created a position for me when I wanted to transfer in. I think it was approved because of that double murder. Jack had to assist the local deputy because he didn't have any experience or support."

Sam grinned at Jack. "I can still remember the day Mick burst into my kitchen to ask for your help. I didn't know you were a medical examiner and was very confused. Then I got angry because I thought you were a policeman and had arrested Melissa."

Listening closely, Tom was spellbound. "I've never heard any of this."

"The three of us haven't really talked. I imagine Jack would like to hear more about Vegas and how we met, too."

"Me too," Minoru said. "Your lives sound so exciting." He thought Santo Milagro might be too small to hire another detective, but he might as well start somewhere he had friends. *Are they my friends?* He thought maybe they were, or they would be.

"It's not all excitement," Tom said. "Some days, I sit in the office or spend hours helping a rancher find a lost cow. Jack's the one with the busy case load."

"You were even busier than me for a lot of years."

Tom nodded. "Tell me, Minoru, why do you want to work in the United States? Is it just the quest for excitement?"

"No. I'm not sure if I can explain it properly. Since I returned from America, I've been treated like an outsider. Sometimes people call me 'gaijin', it means foreigner. The other policemen are polite, but they don't ask me to join them for a drink, and they don't confide in me. More than anything, I want to feel like part of the brotherhood. I feel lonely here."

His admission was met with momentary silence, but then Tom nodded. "I can understand that."

"Won't you miss your family?" Sam asked.

"My father passed away a few years ago in the line of duty. He was a policeman, too. My mother lives in Texas."

"That's why you went to college there?"

"Yes, I miss her." He took a deep breath and said, "I will do it. When can I come?"

"What do you think, Sam?"

"Any time you like. I'll write down our numbers and e-mails, and you just let us know when you can take a vacation." She scribbled on a piece of paper and then passed it to him. "Do you ride horseback?"

"No," he said with surprise. "Is that a requirement?"

"No." She laughed. "Just for fun."

When his new friends finally took their leave, Minoru shook Jack's hand. "I don't know how to thank you, Jack. You may have just changed my life."

"I'm not changing it; *you* are. You took the first step."

"I'm glad you're not angry about the investigation."

"I told you before—there's no place for personal feelings in a murder investigation. My only concern was incarcerating the right person, even if it had been my cousin."

Minoru nodded. "I suspected we had the wrong man, so I continued to investigate even though Fukuda was convinced he would confess."

"You'll be an asset to whatever department you join." Jack clapped him on the shoulder.

"I agree." Tom nodded. "I'll be looking forward to your visit."

Standing in his doorway, Minoru watched them go downstairs and get in the taxi he had called. His spirits soared as he envisioned a bright new future.

Chapter 24

The house was vacant when they returned, so Sam suggested they take Tom to the park. "We never did get to see the little shrines, but after the murder, I felt funny going back there. Also, we can do the 'you know what' again." She didn't want to spoil the surprise for Tom.

"Oh, yeah. The 'you know what'." Jack winked at Sam and grinned.

Tom laughed. "I never know what to expect with you two, but at least I'm being included."

"Are we okay now?" Jack asked him.

"Yes. We're okay. I'm sorry I was such a jerk."

"Ditto."

"Glad that's settled," Sam said. "Let's go."

On their way, Sam pointed out the small temple entrance. "I never got to see it. Can we stop and take a look?"

"Sure. I bet Jack's ancestors are buried here."

They entered through the small gate and came to a basin with water running down a narrow bamboo chute, standing under a small, ornate roof. "This is a ritual cleansing station," Tom told them. "Take the ladle and pour a little water over one hand, then the other." He demonstrated. "Then pour a little in your hand and wet your lips. Rinse the handle and replace it on the rack." He replaced his ladle and said, "Let me ask the priest about your family. Just a second."

After a short conversation, he motioned them to come as he followed the priest through the mostly gray, cubical graves. "Doumo arigato gozaimasu." Tom bowed low to the priest, who smiled pleasantly and bowed.

"This is the Akiyama family plot. Land is dear, so a family will purchase a small square and add names and ashes as family members pass away. I can't read the names, but it looks like there are quite a few. Maybe you can ask your family who's buried here."

"Why are those things sitting on the graves?"

"Families come at certain times and do a ritual cleansing of the grave and leave gifts for the departed. They might leave a pack of cigarettes or a small cup of sake, maybe some flowers or a favorite snack."

After spending a short time looking around the cemetery, the three left through the gate, feeling a little more solemn than when they entered. "I wish I could bring my mother's ashes here to be with her family."

"Where is she buried?"

"I don't know. Father wouldn't allow me to speak of her."

They all remained silent until the park was in sight, and Sam couldn't contain her excitement any longer. Tom and Jack both smiled as she bounced on her toes, waiting for them to catch up. Jack waited as Sam led Tom to the top of the hill and showed him the slide. Then climbed the steps as she went flying down the rollers. Tom gingerly sat on the rollers and let out a shout when Jack gave him an unexpected shove. "Sam, look out!" he yelled as he approached the bottom, and Jack chuckled as he began to slow.

After three trips down the slide, they managed to pry Sam away. Looking back, she said, "Best. Slide. Ever."

"Did you get pictures?"

"You betcha, cuz."

"The last time we came," Jack explained, "we found a dead body on our way to see some shrines. So, we haven't seen the next part yet."

They walked down the wooded path, seemingly innocent and serene, to the end, where five small wooden boxes sat raised off the ground. They were open in the front, covered only by wire mesh. Sam stopped and peered inside one of the boxes.

"I'm a little disappointed. I thought they would be much more ornate."

"Still, kind of cool if you're not expecting to find anything," Tom said.

"I liked the slide better." She grinned. "Ready to head back?"

True to his promise, when they returned from the park, Tom sat with Jack and his grandparents and helped bridge the language barrier. He related what Obaa-san had told him about Jack's mother and interpreted his questions. Then, it was the grandparents' turn.

"What do you remember about your mother?" His grandmother asked.

"After she died, my father wouldn't allow me to mention her, so I began to forget things. This trip has brought back some of my memories. She taught me how to use chopsticks and showed me Japanese children's shows on video. I remember sitting on her bed and watching her brush her long hair, and I remember her hugs. She always let me know I was safe and loved."

"Your father was kind to her?"

"Yes. He found out about my conception on the day she died, so he was grieving her loss but also angry. He never recovered from that."

"At least you had your cousin?"

"I forgot I had a cousin after so many years apart. We were both surprised when we met by accident years later." Jack related the story of how they met when his father, on his deathbed, made him promise to go to Santo Milagro to repay an old debt. "I thought he was sending me to visit an old friend, but it was my uncle. When I arrived, I was met by my cousin, who told me her father had also passed away a year earlier."

Tom was as amazed as Jack's grandparents. "Neither of you remembered?"

"I remembered first, but it took Sam longer.

"She's younger than me and had blocked out the trauma of losing me and her mother at the same time."

"Wait a minute. How did she lose her mother?"

"Our mothers were in the car together when the accident happened. After that day, my father broke all contact with Sam's family. It was like they had never existed."

"I'm sorry we didn't search harder. We should have been there to help."

At the moment Jack saw his grief reflected in his grandmother's eyes, he felt a little piece of his heart return. He recognized his mother in those eyes and knew he had finally found what he was looking for.

<hr>

"Tadaima," Annie called from the entryway.

"Okaerinasai."

"We have a surprise for you this evening, so take a little rest and put on something you want to be seen in."

They entered the guest room and laid in a row on top of their futons. Jack said, "We're leaving early the day after tomorrow. I wonder what they've got planned."

"No telling, but I suppose we're eating out." Sam's stomach rumbled, and Tom laughed.

"Don't laugh. I may have a tapeworm."

"Sorry, dear." He grinned. "She didn't say how long to rest."

"Normal people rest for half an hour. Sam rests for as long as you let her."

"Stop picking on me." She closed her eyes, and the next thing she knew, it was five o'clock, and Annie was tapping on the door.

"Wakey, wakey. Departure time is in half an hour."

Sam sat up and rubbed her eyes. Tom and Jack were gone. *Dang it. They let me sleep.* "What are you wearing?" she called.

Annie opened the door and did a pirouette. Her short-sleeved, navy dress flared around her as she spun.

"You look lovely. I only brought one dress. I don't wear them much."

"No worries. Wear whatever you like. I'll let you be so you can change."

Sam looked through her clothes. She liked dresses on other women, but she never felt comfortable in them. The one she took to Japan with her was a very simple, black, calf-length body-con dress. *I suppose that will be okay.* She put it on and added some very low heels. When she entered the living room, everyone gaped.

"Should I change?"

"No! You look stunning," Annie said.

"Absolutely gorgeous," Jack agreed.

"All I can say is it's lucky you're my wife, or I'd be on the cheatin' train."

"Tom!"

"You're still the most beautiful woman I've ever seen." He kissed her cheek.

Jack rolled his eyes, and Takashi laughed.

"Is everyone ready?"

"Annie makes good tour guide."

She elbowed Takashi and shooed everyone toward the door.

"Where's everyone else?" Sam asked.

"You'll see. Come on."

<hr>

Takashi pulled the minivan into a circular drive. The covered drive was strung with white lights, and a young man in a suit took his keys as everyone disembarked. Taking Annie's arm, Takashi led them through the front doors and into an elegant restaurant. The hostess asked for his name before leading them into the back.

When they entered the private room, they were surprised to find it filled with family and new friends. The Shima family, the Hiranos, and Yoko from English class were in attendance. Oba clapped when they entered, and Jack's grandmother smiled widely.

Finding name cards at the long table, Jack admired the ornate, gold-trimmed plates and gleaming stemware.

"Everything is so beautiful," Sam said.

The four-course, Italian-inspired dinner began with antipasto and was followed by cake. Jack's grandfather stood at the head of the table and raised his glass. Annie interpreted as he spoke.

"We have been so immensely pleased to meet our Sachiko's son, Jack, and to welcome him to the family. It has been a pleasure, Jack, and I hope we will see you many times in the future."

Jack was overwhelmed by the sentiment and the trouble they took, and before he could stop himself, he dashed the moisture from his eyes and approached his grandparents. Throwing his arms around his grandmother, he hugged her. She stiffened for a moment, then hugged him back, holding him tightly. The lump in his throat grew as Grandma, then Oba, then Grandpa, and even Oji hugged him.

His grandfather cleared his throat and took his seat before the bestowing of gifts began.

Jack felt like he should say something grand but had no words. "Doumo arigato gozaimasu," he said, then glancing at Annie so she would interpret, he added, "I don't know what to say. Your generosity and kindness are overwhelming, but the greatest gift is the gift of family. I promise we will have many more visits."

<hr>

When the party was over, and the guests began to disperse, the younger generation continued on to the second party at a local karaoke box, where Takashi had made reservations. Entering the establishment and following a staff member down a long hall, they were ushered inside a small room with comfortable sofas and a table.

"What is this place?" Sam looked around in awe.

"It's a private karaoke party room. We can order food and drinks and sing as much as we like," Annie grinned. "We don't even have to stand on stage; we can just sit where we are and grab a microphone."

"How fun." Sam glanced curiously at Keiko, who had taken a seat next to Jack. *If she sits any closer, she'll be on his lap.*

The staff member returned and took drink orders. "We might want to get some snacks," Annie said, "but I'm completely stuffed right now."

Jack nodded. "Why don't we wait on the snacks." He tried to slide over a little, but Keiko just moved closer.

Takashi was already scrolling through the song index.

"We have another surprise for you, Jack."

His eyebrow rose, and Annie grinned. "We have one more guest."

The server returned with drinks, and Minoru Ito entered behind him.

"Welcome, Inspector," Annie said.

"Please call me Minoru. Thank you for inviting me." He shook hands with Jack and Tom. "What's everyone drinking?"

"Beer mostly. We had quite a bit of wine with dinner," Jack said.

"I have whiskey," Takashi said.

"Whiskey for me too," Minoru told the server, "and yakitori please."

Sam saw Takashi watching him and wondered if he could feel it. *It was nice of them to invite him after everything that happened.*

━━━━•·❦·•━━━━

Minoru did feel Takashi's stare. The waves of distrust and... not anger, but certainly negative emotion, were almost palpable. It was not customary for policemen to apologize for any actions taken in the line of duty, but he felt he must say something to clear the air. Once the drinks were delivered, he took his and sat in the space next to Takashi.

Speaking quietly in Japanese, he said, "I understand how you feel. It was very kind of you to invite me this evening."

"That was a difficult situation. Did you really think I killed him with my own mother's scarf?"

"I continued investigating because I suspected you weren't our man."

"I can't believe Akio-kun is a murderer. I have known him my entire life."

"He wanted to protect his mother."

Takashi gave a brief nod. "You aren't like other policemen, are you?"

"In some ways, I am. I can't apologize for doing my job, but I am truly sorry for what you went through. It is never our intention to persecute the innocent."

"Thank you. Somehow, that helps." The muscles in his face and shoulders relaxed as he held up his glass and clinked it against Minoru's. "Kampai."

"Kampai." Minoru rose and returned to his seat next to Tom.

Without looking at him, Tom said, "You're a good man, Ito."

"Have you ever been the lone dissenting voice when the evidence is pointing to someone you think is innocent?"

"I have. Not very often, though. Law enforcement isn't just a job; it's the deep-seated need to uphold justice. Sometimes, it can be a lonely road."

Chapter 25

Breakfast had come and gone by the time Sam woke. Alone in the guestroom, she got dressed and wandered into the living room. Annie was sitting at the table and asked if she'd like some coffee.

"Yes, please. Where is everyone?"

"Golden Week is over, so everyone is back to work. Jack and Tom went to the bento kitchen with Takashi and his father. Etsuko-san took Grandma to the hair salon. Ji-ji went to one of his friends' houses. I don't know what they get up to." She shrugged. "Would you like to go to the supermarket so you can buy the things you want to take home with you?"

"That would be great. I can't believe our trip is over already." Sam shook her head. "It went by so quickly."

Annie went into the kitchen and returned with coffee and toast. "Takashi and I thought we would drive you to the airport in the morning."

"Isn't it awfully far?"

"A little, yes, but we'd like to see you off. Did you mean it when you invited me to visit your ranch?"

"Yes! Absolutely. Jack won't be there, though, unless he drives up for a weekend."

"I talked to Takashi like you suggested. He said that moving to Australia, however temporary, is probably not an option, but he understands how I feel and suggested that I take you up on your offer. I was angry at first, but then I thought about it and realized that it might be just what I need."

Munching on her toast, Sam gazed at Annie.

201

"It might. Just getting away from the routine, experiencing something new, being among people who speak the same language… more or less." She grinned.

"You really wouldn't mind?"

"Not at all. I love having company. Although, I won't be waiting on you. That is way too much pressure."

"We were talking about that too. I told him I don't want to turn into his mother, and he gets that. I don't know what we'll do about it, but I suppose when I get back, I should talk to Etsuko about my feelings and see what she has to say. Even though she takes her responsibilities seriously, she's surprisingly open to new ideas."

"I like her. Maybe you should bring her with you."

Annie sat very still. "It's a thought." Pausing, she said, "Even though I like her a lot, I really want to get away from it all."

"Maybe you can come on your own this time, and the family can plan a future trip. Everyone could come for Thanksgiving or Christmas, or even in the summer if they'd prefer nice weather."

Relaxing, Annie grinned. "You have the best ideas. Where would you like to eat lunch?"

Jack had entered the room and laughed. "I thought Sam was the only one who planned lunch while she was eating breakfast."

"Oh, ha ha."

"Why don't you two have bento lunch with the rest of the family? Then Takashi said he'll show us where the myoga grow."

"Deal. Did you want to go with us to the supermarket? Sam wants to pick up a few food items to take home."

"No, I'll stay with the menfolk." Jack winked.

"Write down those recipes, cuz. I'm going to need them."

Jack left, and Annie poured more coffee. "Do you have a list of things you'd like to buy?"

"Not really. Japanese mayonnaise, mirin, dashi, curry rue…"

"Bulldog sauce!"

"Oh, yeah. And what's in the gyouza sauce?"

"Hot sesame oil—rayu."

"That too. Am I missing anything?"

"I don't know. We can go up and down the aisles and see if we notice anything good."

<hr>

Returning with two shopping bags filled with a variety of foods, seasonings, and snacks, Sam looked at her overflowing suitcase and sighed. Annie left the room and returned with a large, red suitcase. "You can use this for your extra stuff."

"No, I couldn't. I should have bought one."

"I can bring it back with me when I find myself in the same situation."

Hugging her, Sam said, "Thank you. You're so clever. I was wondering what I would have to leave behind."

Annie helped her pack and looked up when the men returned for lunch.

"Tadaima."

"Okaeri," she and Sam called.

Takashi, Jack, and Tom placed obento boxes around the dining table, and Oji roared, "Gohan!"

Etsuko bustled into the room, followed by Jack's freshly coifed grandmother.

As everyone found their places around the table, Takashi said, "Our visiting chefs helped prepare our lunch today. Thank you, Jack and Tom."

They took small, mock bows and joined the others.

Opening her box, Obaa-san said, "Oishisou."

Everyone murmured agreement that it looked delicious. Yaki onigiri, grilled rice balls in honor of Sam, accompanied Jack's favorite, gomae, and Tom's, kinpira gobo. Takashi had added yaki soba and chicken karaage as the protein.

"Maybe not traditional food combo, but everyone's favorites. Itadakimasu."

"So good." Sam savored everything. "Will we have recipes?"

"I wrote down every word," Tom assured her.

"Did we buy karaage seasoning?"

"Yes, I figured you would want it, even though it wasn't on your list." Annie smiled at her.

After lunch, Takashi took them for a walk on the beach, where he showed them how to find wild myoga. The tops looked like weeds poking out of the sand. Sam thought they were beautiful, three or four inches long and streaked with pink and green. *They look like some kind of exotic flower.*

She scanned the beach, trying to memorize the feel of the cool breeze and the smell of the ocean. It was a lonely beach. She wondered if it got busier during the summer. "It was pure luck that Hannah was here that morning," she murmured.

Standing by her side, Tom glanced at her.

"It's always deserted."

"Do you think they arranged to meet here?" he whispered.

"No, I think it was just dumb luck."

Takashi held up a few myoga. "I put in soup tonight," he announced.

"Speaking of which, we'll have to leave at two in the morning, so do you want to take a nap? Go to bed very early? Not sleep at all?" Annie asked.

"I don't know about everyone else, but I don't know if I'll be able to sleep."

"You will," Jack and Tom said in unison, then burst into gales of laughter.

"I hate you both." Sam pretended to pout. "Can we take one last walk to the park, to the slide, then nap?"

"Or we could just go to bed early and sleep a little less than usual," Jack suggested. "We'll probably be able to sleep on the plane."

"That sounds good to me," Tom said. "Are we all on the same flight?"

"Yes, I have great organizational skills."

"You do, actually." Tom smiled.

"I will defer to our great planners… as long as I get to go down that slide a couple more times."

"I go back to work. See you at dinner." Takashi left them in front of the house.

<hr>

It was a bittersweet dinner, sometimes boisterous and sometimes introspective. Oji brought out the sake again, and Tom helped Jack speak with his grandparents. They all took turns in the bath and retired early so they could rise well before dawn.

As he lay in his futon for the final time, Jack thought over his visit, picturing scenes with his family members. He pictured their first meeting, his anger at Takashi's dismissal, walking arm in arm with his grandmother, their hugs at his going-away party, and he was filled with an indefinable feeling; he thought it might be akin to a feeling of belonging. Not the sense of community he felt in Santo Milagro, because his cultural ignorance set him apart. *It's more like knowing I came from here, and these people care about me.* His father's rejection and his lack of family growing up had left an open wound. Reuniting with Sam had helped, but after this trip, he thought he might be able to heal. His mind drifted to Sam and her willingness to join him on this trip, even though it caused strife at home. And Tom, so patient and understanding. He was grateful to them both. *I need to be a better friend, less selfish.* He finally drifted off to sleep with a smile on his face.

<hr>

Alarms echoed through the house at one o'clock in the morning. Sam bounced out of bed and threw on her clothes before closing up her suitcase one final time. "Up and at 'em, sleepyheads."

It seemed to her that every light in the house was on, and upon entering the living area, she was surprised to see Etsuko fully dressed and carrying plates of toast to the table.

The rest of the family came shuffling in, one at a time.

"Ohayou gozaimasu," they said as they entered.

Everyone was seated by one-twenty, and they sat quietly. "I wish you could stay longer," Annie said wistfully. "I've really enjoyed your visit."

"It's been amazing. I can't wait to come again. And you'll be visiting us soon, right?" Sam said.

"Yes." Annie glanced at Takashi. "You meant it, right?"

Smiling at her, he nodded. "I don't lie."

Before Sam knew it, their suitcases had been loaded into the minivan, and Jack bowed low to the elder family members. To her surprise, Obaa-san approached him and tentatively put her arms around him. She was followed by the others as they forewent their usual stoicism and let him know how much they loved him. Turning away, she dashed at her eyes.

They climbed into the minivan and waved until they could no longer see the Akiyama house. Sam's eyes slowly drifted closed as she leaned against Tom, his even breathing and familiar voice lulling her into a peaceful sleep.

Mother of two, cat mom, and prolific reader, Alice Kanaka is the author of six traditional mysteries, seven short stories, and a twelve-episode collaboration with Black Knight, author of the *Starshatter* space opera series.

Alice holds a bachelor's degree in Spanish and a Master of Business Administration with a concentration in Human Resources. She spent twelve years working at a state psychiatric hospital, speaks three languages, and has lived in seven countries.

A life-long fan of the mystery genre, Alice's books combine traditional tropes with contemporary characters to create whodunits that are simultaneously familiar and unique. Her aspiration is to write books that she would enjoy reading; stories that are both entertaining and uplifting, perfect with a cup of Earl Grey and a roaring fire on a gloomy day.

HTTPS://AliceKanaka.com

Dear Reader,

Thank you very much for taking the time to read *The Cardinal & the Crane*. This book contains some of my own experiences as a young English teacher in Japan and writing it evoked memories I had nearly forgotten. I hope you enjoyed reading it as much as I enjoyed writing it.

Please be sure to support my author journey by leaving a brief review on Amazon, Goodreads, or your favorite bookseller so more lovely readers like you are able to find my books.

With love and appreciation,

Alice Kanaka